Dear Hugh,

Such a joy to inscribe my book! Thank you for your support and prayers —

Robbie

We Have
a Pie

by
Robert McVey

Livingston Press
The University of West Alabama

Copyright © 2012 Robert McVey
All rights reserved, including electronic text
isbn 13: 978-1-60489-095-2 library binding
isbn 13: 978-1-60489-096-9 trade paper
Library of Congress Control Number 2012930431
Printed on acid-free paper.
Printed in the United States of America,
Publishers Graphic
Hardcover binding by: Heckman Bindery

Typesetting and page layout: Joe Taylor
Cover design and layout: Joe Taylor
Cover art: Leonardo DaVinci, Dover Publications
Cover Photo: Emily Mills Burkett
Proofreading: Christin Loehr, Joe Taylor, Tricia Taylor.

This collection was a runner-up in
the Tartt First Fiction Award,
sponsored in part by The President's Office at UWA.

Livingston Press is part of The University of West Alabama,
and thereby has non-profit status.
Donations are tax-deductible:
brothers and sisters, we need 'em.

first edition
6 5 4 3 2 1

Contents

Part One: 1 ½ - 12

Part Two: 15 - 25

Part Three: 31 ~ 40

Part Four: 41 ~ 50

Part Five: 51 ~ 60

Part Six: 61 ~ Ta-Ta

For Sharon, Sharal, and Reuben

We Have
a Pie

Part One: 1 ½ - 12

Sweetie Is Alright

An abused child's future is like considering an abstract painting, the meaning you make is particular to the way you think. I watched a mother and her year-and-a-half-old son, I'm a friend of another branch of the family. "I'll hold it, sweetie!" she said to him on Christmas morning, holding the bottle, tipping it back so that he might drink his fill. I noticed that his hands were not trying for the bottle with the vigor I had seen even a month ago at Thanksgiving. His movements now were fitful, his body slumped into itself, the mouth a stuck-open hole as it received its milk straight, held by a strong hand. "He'd like to hold it himself," I remarked. She looked at me wonderingly. "What child wouldn't like his mother to hold his bottle?" The baby whimpered. "Oh, are you alright, sweetie?" the mother asked. Her vowels were elongated, her consonants were gluey. By the Christmas tree, the year-and-a-half-old sat staring into space and made his sound with the mother, having gone to a side table for a salted nut, crying and breaking through people to get to him. "He seems very attached to you," said an appalled guest. "Yes, it's very flattering," she said. She's flattered? We watched the baby lose life. It was possible her son would grow up and be a pro-wrestler, but not with that increasingly translucent skin. Does a network of veins at a baby's temple increase in visibility as his spirit fades? I know that the mother sleeps with the baby in the bed, and the father parked on the sofa. If it weren't for those gluey consonants and elongated vowels, I might have attempted a pardon, but no, she wants to entomb her child within herself, infanticide, not with a golf club, ball-peen hammer, rug beater, male member, it's shapeless, moist, enveloping, it's a mist upon my vitals. I am at risk this Christmas morn. Nor am I alone. A four-year-old visitor lurches in terror to escape from all people, change species, if she can. The father begins to call his son "sweetie," a nascent quick eunuch bloomed in time-elapsed photography screech. A woman feels she has an incurable food addiction, back of a slice of fruit cake. A young cousin loses his purity at table, craves drugs, wants to talk dirty, direct music videos. The baby's eyes are now only half-open. He's emitting a sound that doesn't rise to the level of whimper. She says "swee," but doesn't get to the second syllable. I reach for a knife blindly.

We Have a Pie

My Breathing Bothered My Mother

My breathing bothered my mother as we took our afternoon nap together, so I had to turn my body away from hers and was miserable about it. It occurs to me, generations later, that if she had thought to insert some piece of cloth between my nostril holes and whatever part of her body my air was landing on, then she could have slept and I could have continued to have been related to. For want of a nail. We were not naked ~ I believe I had on a white tee-shirt and briefs and she a pink knee-length nightie. Her breasts were so soft. I don't remember minding her breathing. This was the place I belonged. It was quiet and still in the house. My brother and sister in school, my father at work. I can remember trying to stop breathing so I wouldn't have to turn. I remember craning my neck to put my head someplace else, but flesh never gives enough. Before it all went to pieces, everything contributed to the mood of intimate repose I so needed. A gray cold winter day making the bedroom almost dark; cool smooth satiny blankets for both of us to get under, we, there, warm planet. Before she climbed in, I might have held out a bottle of vanilla extract for her to dab behind each ear, winking as she did so. In the event, I would hum the first measures to the theme song of *The Flintstones* while she removed a bobby pin or two. It became a tepid affair with her preference of my rear end in her middle. But the law of life did not apply to me every day I have lived. I'll remember about the cloth. I believe other sticking points will be dealt with as they appear. Every problem has a simple solution, if only thought of.

Green Lights

"Look at that fat man," one child cried to some of the others on the school bus, and they looked out the bus window and saw through the front window of the car below the gut of a fat man as he sat and angrily waited for the light to change. One of the children recognized him as his father. All the other children laughed. "Look at him!" "Look at it move!" "He's a pig!" They oinked and snuffled to each other. The fat man's kid made himself invisible. Children can do that. They can fly, too. And discover secret passages to away to in their homes. They also can pretend they're other people's children, but that's a flight which the fat man's kid refused to undertake. At home, the fat man ate into immobility. A red light was hardly the only stop signal that enraged him. "Why won't you put out?" he asked his wife in front of the television, "you're a bitch." "You're a fat pig, and I'm sorry I married you," she replied. "Then get the fuck out if you don't like it, let's see who you're giving head to by this time next week." The kid and his twin sister scrunched their noses with distaste at this, showing each other. Not that they understood "put out" or "give head," thinking maybe it was "extending a helping hand" or "kissing" ~ who knew? And who cared? Who wanted to understand what the fat pig said? They got on their bicycles and rode, not answering their mother's harassed questions behind them. The sun was going down. They threw themselves into leaf piles. "Let's bring some leaves back to Daddy," his sister said. They still both hoped beauty could make life beautiful. They flew. That night the air was so dry actual little sparks flew as well, in the darkness from blankets as they snapped with electricity. He slept with his sister. They were indifferent to their different bodies now, like two co-habiting dogs that no longer sniff. Neither dreamed of their parents. Children can do that too. The father dreamed of his family. They were in a sleek sedan never stopping with perfume from his wife intoxicating them all, and all their smiling never stopped as well.

*

La Monstrua

I had wanted for years to see the portraits of La Monstrua, and finally at the Guggenheim Museum's show of Spanish art got my chance; but even I had not known her story, which was told in the exhibition art book, of how she was so amazingly fat at the age of eight that her parents had brought her to the Spanish court to present her to the king and to ask him: you want her? And the king had said, "Of course!" and the parents left her, and the king put her in his retinue of dwarves, freaks and idiots and had her portrait done two times. I looked at her portraits done by the Apelles of the Spanish court, the one of a fleshy head popped on top of a barrel body covered in vast red brocade ironic in its lavishness, each hand holding food; the other naked. None of the other dwarves, freaks and idiots in the exhibition were naked, and none were female; I hoped she understood the rules. For her nakedness, one of her hands held an ironic unnatural flowering plant which thinly curled in front of her; the Apelles obscured her aperture. Her blotted dark eyes were hazy in their misery in both paintings. I had sought her out the way one looks for people beyond help. Now it was all over. She had grown old and died, or at any rate died. Her misery was infinite in her moment in time which was a past moment. I could be wrong, she could have had a lovely life at court and appreciated it all the more for her rocky beginnings, but at the end of the day

I feel safe in my estimation of the joy she had on the planet. I noticed some other people looking at the portraits. In particular, a woman's face was a study in compassion. But she wasn't even there at the deathbed, so it doesn't count.

Dauphin

Please don't whip the dauphin. He is nine years old. You are chasing him around a stone cell with birch branches in your hand. His arms are raised to block the blows, but there is nowhere for him to run. Someone is making a sketch of it.

He was born in a palace and nursed by Madame Poitrine. He was painted by Vigée Le Brun. Scotty Beckett played him in the real movie. But that was then and this is now.

He was made to testify that he had had carnal knowledge of his mother, Marie-Antoinette. He was taught to sing dirty songs. Two hundred years later, an article in the *Times* said he had had an eye put out. He was made tubercular. He was made insane. His pickled heart was found in a jar on a shelf. DNA testing proved it was his, ripped from his chest.

And was he forced to eat feces? Can you feel the fingers at his nape forcing the head down? And did he form himself into a ball from the blows, and come to croon as the faster flagellation stage arrived? I can hear it, can you?

He was spoiled for life before he was death-smashed. The day came when he was primed ever to destroy beings weaker than he. He had become a serpent in its egg. No. Riesener furniture or tuberose perfume memory cannot be supplanted. At this point it was better that he should go.

A faraway bird calls. He hears it, and his one eye shines

bright. For some reason he is biting off his own left forefinger. The bird flies away with it after it is thrown by the other hand out the cell window. He will be the bird's food. Nothing is left but scraps, and he knows it.

He sinks to his knees with the administered deathblow. There are no thoughts of his mother. Not even the stone floor is hard. A fever sleep fills his head. His death year will have a question mark. The jailer is hoping for a death fart. As ever, he was not disappointed.

Melanie Klein Said

The psychoanalyst Melanie Klein said that life itself is an aberration. Now that's going for it. I believe when she was a child, she was blamed for her brother's death by her parents, but, as always, I haven't looked into the matter. But do not one and one make two in this instance? On the whole, per Melanie Klein, there should be only rocks and not even lichen on them to achieve a true state of nature, and so maybe she did kill him, and then said to her parents, doubting Thomases heretofore of her precept, "There, see what I mean?" But this was not to be my way. I stood in front of the class at age nine with a crayon drawing of a burning house and put my forefinger through a crayoned second-story window and cried, "Help, help, help!," wiggling the finger wildly. The teacher had told us to do drawings for a little girl named Anita, who had been burned out of her home last week in Philadelphia. It had been in the papers. She would be sent the drawings. Mine was a lively art, not like Melanie's demonstration. But what would it be like if any children were able to say at such a juncture, "What in God's name are crayon drawings made by strangers going to do for a homeless child? Do you think Anita wants to reflect on twenty-eight versions of the inferno from which she somehow escaped with her life? Is your intention to traumatize and retraumatize this child twenty-eight-fold, courtesy of Crayola? Or does it go deeper than that, are you demonstrating for Anita your belief in Freud's concept of the death instinct, Miss Neary? Are you attempting via artwork to induce in this child a regret that she ignored her unconscious urge to run back into the flames? In this attempt, are you using us as your cat's paw? Did you know Melanie Klein said life itself is an aberration?" One by one we all got in front of the class and showed our drawings. Mine was the only one which had a body part bursting out a window. Maybe from that I could have gone on to become a full-blooded male, a Jackson Pollack type, or, if not an artist, a hardass prosecutor type, or a soldier-of-fortune reporter type drunkenly heckling photo-op politicos in a war zone. But this as it happened was my high tide. I think it was Anita's, too. I think Anita burned her own house down, and I hope she did. No school for her the next day. No fish on Friday. Daddy's filthy porn an ash. Not only living things can be destroyed, Melanie. Everything can go, and people can live free, Miss Neary: Anita's Law.

We Have a Pie

Mom Was Trussed

Mom was trussed with her own clothesline and stashed in the bedroom. Sis was pinioned and thrust headfirst in the clothes hamper, Mary Janes extended, kicking helplessly in the air. Junior was lashed to the leg of the dining room table, working buttocks against the floor in a fruitless frenzy to Escape and Tell. Dad was viciously blackjacked by the carport, then hog-tied by one who knew how so very well, the kind of knots which only tightened if met with resistance. All four mouths were stopped by triangles of handkerchief gags knotted at the nape. Urgent pre-electronic music ground on through the sequence as the house was ransacked, then burnt.

I had two parents and a sister and was of the male gender and, age twelve, lived in a house. I watched the TV show avidly, pleased at the perfection that not one family member was uncaught and unbound, then was indifferent at the several rescues, water douses, and final group rejoicing.

Now, today, I watched a 101-year-old woman get punched in the face repeatedly. This was black-and-white film too, you'd think security cameras would be upgraded to color by now. But I should start at the beginning. The sequence ["Violence in America" on CNN] began with a car door opening and a slob piling out and firing a pistol in the direction of the camera filming him. Then it moved on to two teenage girls kicking the head of a third as she lay on the ground. Next, a kid was beaten with a baseball bat, the bat was all of the agent of violence you saw, it hit him several times in the trunk and head ~ an immediacy in the point of view. Then there was violence in the discount store, two fat people with their hands on the forearms of each other whirling themselves down the sneaker aisle. Then the 101-year-old got hers. Then a man beat up his wife while she tried to get her licks in. It was all on one half of the screen while on the other half an expert responded to the usual questions of a broadcast journalist. I mostly watched it with the sound off, and supplied my own faint music track, which I had to adjust to a repeat chorus in recognition of seeing the slob pile out of the car again with his pistol blazing again. These acts of violence had been placed on an endless loop. Teenage kicked-head girl, baseball bat-dented kid, K-Mart mayhem, the triple digit lady, Mr. and Mrs. Punch and Judy, slob out of car, etc. I wasn't avid now, and in fact my view of myself after a lifetime of this is that I haven't been degraded at all. This is a triumph of the human spirit. I'd even like to find someone to love.

We Have a Pie

Part Two: 15 - 25

Make a Note

My aunt who was raising me said I was a pig, and I said I wished she'd die. I was fifteen, and she had cancer. It was terminal; that's why I said it. I went to my room and turned to page one of my *Cours de philosophie*. Philosophy has two senses, one, from the most distant time, that of a vision of the world, the other, more recent, now that we were in an age of reason, of a *critical reflection* of those themes which in the distant time made up the vision of the world.

She drank her beer and had her cigarette as she called out to me that I was filthy. I called back that I knew. The second point made in my philosophy book was that philosophy is more or less consonant with the time and place in which it is formed, a part of the human culture in which it arises.

My aunt screamed. I ran to her, crying. It was a jolt from her tumor. These jolts happen, they pass. On the television a blond man was roughing up a blonde woman in that fake soap opera way. Both my aunt and I knew the real thing. We smirked, looking at the screen. "Paste her one," my aunt said to the man.

I went back to my room. Point three was that "culture" is not to be differentiated from "civilization," as the Germans, the French book said severely, are wont to do ~ I enjoy any prejudice, any hate ~ *both* are organically, closely aligned in any time and place.

I heard her beer belch from the next room. I said, Who's a pig. She said, Fix your hair, whore. She objected to my hair, which was teased "like a teenage Jezebel." I told her I was a teenage Jezebel. She said more lezzy than jezzy. I told her she was right and to go fuck herself. I walked out to give her the finger.

She asked for a kiss, which I gave her, withstanding the beer breath, sores, and touch of the tubes going into her nose. I asked her if her life had been happy. She said that I was her happiness. I wanted her to say more. She said she would tomorrow, but she died the next day. There was a main thought, in any case.

Brandon's Body

"When I'm on the subway, my insides start shaking. My nails are growing, I'm not biting them, but I pick my face. I say to myself it's to open my pores, I want open pores, that's why I pop my blackheads, but it leaves a mark, so I know it makes no sense and at other times, to be totally honest, I just pick. No, I won't say there's a relief after a good pick, that's too weird. Let's just say I have a habit."

He looks at me with the unfinished face of a twenty-year-old. He arose from red state stupidity, now New York has left an effect of knowing a Project Runway contestant, tee-shirt cool logos, and yoga mats. Yes, he does say, "It sucks to be positive, ma'am."

He wants to see Ricky, who infected him, to comfort him because Ricky wants to die now, being positive. The adolescent thus shows that he knows more about love than I do, a fact which I do not allow to show on my homely face. What do I call Ricky: the 'young man' who infected him, the 'lover' who infected him, the 'boy' who infected him, the 'male' who infected him? I suppose feelings from questions like that lead politicians to list Ricky, cage Ricky, defame Ricky, defund Ricky, get elected on the strength of and then ignore Ricky.

He has a pill bottle in his hand and points to it with the other, like an old-fashioned endorsement ad. "Maybe I'm the one that medication doesn't work on, you never know, I could be, well, that's life." We are definitely at the how-will-I-tell-my-mother stage of life, definitely at the trying-to-summon-up-adolescent-simplicity-and-grace in the death-be-not-proud stage of life. He's got a Harry Potter in his bag. He likes to read when it rains. Returns to Ricky, no tears, but voice husky. I'm present in my separateness.

"How can I calm down? That's what I want to know. Do you have any ideas?"

Absolutely not. "I always think these things are best done in a simple way. Just close your eyes and breathe deeply." I close my eyes and demonstrate a breath, my spread fingers in front of my chest to indicate my lungs, my well lungs. "Just breathe in ~ no stomach breaths ~ breathe into your lungs ~ and out. And again. And again. Concentrate on your breath. Breathe to your core. You probably won't need to do it for a long time. I'm not saying do this for an hour. Probably a few minutes. You'll know when to stop. Your body will tell you."

*

An Off Night

She came, she saw, she schnorred. I'm not good enough for her, but on a rainy weekday night she'll extend her dinner plate toward the chili pot wherein I have prepared my evening meal. She'll gussy up the schnorr by bright small talk ~ that's to promote the fiction that we're two equals, each hungry, supporting our corporeal beings in tandem ~ only I provide all, I always provide all. All but that beautiful face. That is what I am to adore of her. Whether I do or not is a secret I try to believe is locked in my heart.

She asks about my day. As I begin, she looks at the time on her wristwatch. Luckily the wrist she rotates is not the one attached to the hand holding the plate of chili, or the schnorred food would go ker-plop all down her preppy tartan p.j.'s

It's forever advisable to have her speak instead, it's arresting too, since she's always in situations where people act differently from any human behavior I've ever seen. People are always breathless at family tradition around the dinner table in Cos Cob, or people on a boat are always teetering, struck dumb by the seascape off Martha's Vineyard, something or other is always a hoot, Republicans always have the good of everyone in mind, one's Chamber of Commerce, if anything, cares too much ~ there's always a passion party going down in places I have no access.

I wish it were real. Scratch that, I wish there were even a scrap of truth. It would help her too. I recognize it's tough when your mother gets drunk and walks out of her room showing her twat. Pulls down her sweats. Does it a lot. Headband still in place. In fact, I don't recognize clearly how tough that is.

I don't think that she's necessarily destined to be more of a lost soul than I am. Grimness exacts its price. Toughness leads to its own form of putrefaction. She goes on about how important living here is for her, what role I play in her life now. This is a staple of her conversation. The "now" addendum is inevitable, almost honest, the temporary caravansary of it all. This is her Peace Corps placement, I am her world experience, it is for me to be doe-eyed though fly-blown.

But then, I rented to her thinking she would be my finishing school. I'd finally get a death grip on French phonetics. Prettiness would engender prettiness. I'd be ~ wait for it ~ socially select. When I realize I might be experiencing the real world instead, there are no words to express my deep gratitude.

Reality Show

A Chinese woman has hanged herself, but my friend said I shouldn't send her son a sympathy card, the vibe seemed to be that it wouldn't be cool. I get it, my friend wants to surround himself with winners. Her son had been one of these. The lady with the bent neck is not. My best guess is she couldn't take it anymore.

My friend's corporation has supplied him with a one-bedroom, a real one-bedroom in a great building. I walk in and say, "I'm jealous." I've been processed by my corporation and not been given a one-bedroom, and I start next week, and I have to scramble. The Chinese dude had a good deal going for himself too. But she probably couldn't stand the last stages of capitalism. All that is solid hangs in the air!

Well, it's the only (living) game in town. But something in me has to send a card. I write, "Just to let you know you're in my thoughts during this time" on an understated card (hard to find in these prole cheap emotion times) and send it out. When it's mailed, I'm glad, but I agree with my friend, emotions are ungainly. To the sender and to the receiver. Receipt of the card demands an emotional heft, a moral compass, on the part of the Chinese dude, which few possess. He may vow my destruction, this vow wafting into key corner offices interconnected with my own, with career track fallout. On the other hand, he may take to sleeping on my doormat at my front door (not paid for by my corporation, I can't believe it) each night curled in gratitude. And I have to admit after sending the card, I did a little research on probability of offspring suicide following parental suicide. Who's weakening is always relevant.

I tell my friend I've sent the card. I do this rather than have the Chinese dude sell me out by telling him. My friend says, a card about what? What a business head! I tell him. He seems indifferent, but between this false move and my not being rewarded with a one-bedroom by my corporation, it looks like my fate is sealed, like on a reality show when one of the contestants has too much camera time, you know it's the end, though my friend did like my jealousy.

*

Friday Night

There was a moose head with antlers on the wall and a pitcher of beer on the table with the spirited waiter plunking down the platters of veggie burgers and the Red Sox wearing green jackets on the t.v., and an old woman with her old dog sitting on the stoop outside, next to this dive with Friday night people running up and down the block on their way to, or from, drinks. Back inside, the table of people who would never actually make it in the theater world were creating their after-showcase performance conviviality. There was a lesbian, a gay man, a Rabelaisian straight man, a cool cruel straight man, two unpretty straight women and a young man who began talking about his half-sister who had been murdered in the U.K. It became a crazy-person moment, then eternity. Her husband, of course, had killed her. Another half-sister was left in the U.K. She asked her father, now in the U.S., to be with her during the murder trial. All indications were that this was going to be a protracted trial, so the father said he couldn't get off from work. This caused a permanent fissure between them from then on, the young man said. Then the father developed colon cancer. (None of the people hearing this had known the young man for more than ten rehearsals.) The father's second wife, never pleasant at the best of times, left him. The young man himself saw his father as little as possible. His half-sister did not make the trip from the U.K. When the father died, he added. People around the table glanced at each other during the lengthy, then endless, story, timing this so as not to be seen by the young man, fearing a crazed response. There was more and then more, divorces, estrangements, betrayals, disinheritances, all presented chronologically so that at least people could know how far they were from the present year and hopefully know how much longer this would take. There were no other murders, and finally the young man got everyone caught up with his family. No one had any questions, but the Rabelaisian straight man said, with gesticulations, that the young actor was a modern-day Everyman. The lesbian and the gay man made their excuses and admired on the street the dog of the old woman on the stoop. The cool cruel straight man had looked at the confessor with veiled contempt, but, an alcoholic, concentrated on his drinking. The two unpretty straight women had erotic, yet rather pallid, desires for the cool cruel straight man ~ each had a trust fund and knew prettiness was not, for them, in this, a *sine qua non*. The young man now was silent and turned to his cold veggie burger, watching the Red Sox wind up the game, thinking it was getting to be time for him to start home.

The Business

The young lesbian wanted to be liked. The old rich woman did not like her. The not-young, not-old gay man witnessed both facts and was powerless to change this unfortunate dynamic. The old woman did like the gay man. His hair was pretty. He smiled at her. The gay man was nice to the old woman because it was his job. Also, he liked being liked as one whose group is so often not liked can like it. And he appreciated the riches of bright jewelry and dress displayed by the rich woman, he appreciated a life made into spectacle, but it was not an overpowering degree of appreciation. He liked the young lesbian a lot. She was so intent on making good at the job and so unfailingly attentive to clients and to him. She was a moral being who hoped for a reasonable reception from the world. She was not being liked now and felt it as one whose group is so often not liked can feel it. She wanted to be liked by the old rich woman, but she herself did not like her, and she was ashamed of what she did feel. Spoiled, decadent, self-indulgent, useless, parasitic, unfair, demanding, vacuous, were some of the adjectives spooling by on the crawl in her mind during business meetings as she was trying to be liked and listened to by the client. The rich woman did not pay attention much to her own dislike of the young lesbian, was rather vague about it to herself, an unimportant detail in the day of someone who need not put herself in any disliked group, and whose attention, so fallibly, was liable to wander.

It would all be lived out. The young lesbian would spend much time in trying to solve the conundrum of how to be liked as one whose group is so often not liked can try to solve conundrums. This expense of time would enter into an interplay with vibrant unspoken hatred which would contain an element of self-blame, someday perhaps to be mastered. The not-old, not-young gay man would master more easily an impulse of impatience felt towards his supervisee in light of the situation, knowing that the rich woman whom he'd hoped to shift onto his supervisee's workload would still be coming to him for her business. The old rich woman would continue on, smiling or not, listening or not, to whom she pleased or not, and when she pleased or not, and as long as the gay man had pretty hair and sparkling eyes reflecting her jewelry, her business to him as an afternoon part of her life would certainly continue, might even increase.

Part Three: 31 - 40

*

L'Inconnue

In the Louvre I came across a Roman portrait bust, 130 A.D., labeled *Inconnue*, "unknown woman." There were many *inconnues* in the hall, and some *inconnus* as well ~ even for the males it's been two thousand years, and although attention must be paid, really it can't be for all the people.

A poetess ~ on her sculpted throat was a sculpted cameo with a little figure holding a wreath, and the museum sign said this iconography showed that she had won a poetry competition 1,875 years ago. Her eyes were sculpted huge, indicating poetic ecstasy, the sign said. She looked frail and sensitive, central casting got it right. But what was her name and what had she written, what had been her take on life?

With any gift of sight at all, she must have known she was a woman who had to go. And so she rubbed her mouth with a knuckle of her hand as she composed her visions and sang her song against unstoppable oblivion. Then she moved as a living work of art down the streets of Rome to embody her ecstasy, gave it the substance of reality for the time it was given to her and given to all of us. She never brushed against anyone in the street, and in her containment hoped for corresponding wholeness in the receipt and survival of her work, but knew this was a futile wish. The older women who had tried it told her so, and more importantly showed her so. Yet everything in the plethora was so large and endless to her it only seemed logical to think her piece put in could find a place as well. She smiled as she wrote, really as the portrait bust captured it, knowing logic had nothing to do with what she faced.

*

Auto Repair

This is a woman who is sleeping with a twenty-three year-old who does auto repair, and she's thirty-one. She thinks he's too good for her, she has low self-esteem, which means she doesn't like her body, breasts sag, fat on thighs, etc., and it doesn't help she's 4'11". "Why are you looking at other women?" she asks. They watch porn when they copulate. When he's not around she watches it by herself. She's joined a gym to tone her lower half and raise her breasts. She met him in a lounge. They copulated that night. Her friends say she can do better. She knows friends always say you can do better. And then she says to him she has more education and has done more traveling, knowing he'll say what he says, "Yeah, but you're old, you're an old woman." He preens in front of the mirror. He just left his mother and grandmother, got a place of his own. He got it two years into their relationship and did not propose she live with him. She wants children ~ he doesn't. He fathered one at sixteen and has a monthly bill. Neither of them has an interest in this child ~ its mother is raising it. The thirty-one year-old woman is an elementary school teacher. Her disapproving friends are teachers too, but at the end of the day she knows she's the one with the hot stud in the bed, and the rest go home to comfort-eating. They mostly despise their pupils. He wants to own a shop. She never reads a book. She has a vague memory of her father hitting her mother. She lived with her uncle for a year when she was a college student, but he kept telling her what to do. She had a long distance relationship with a Uruguayan. She was thinner then, of course. She had an abortion at nineteen. Her doctor just said she'd better start having children before thirty-five to lessen the chance of birth defects. Her one allowance to self-pity is she wishes at times the Uruguayan would come back, when she knows he won't. She knows no one with whom she can partner in the next few years to give her these kids. She doesn't know how many she wants or why she wants them. What she enjoys is a quick sneer at her friends as she leaves them for the night to go back to the auto repair guy. Actually, it's her only enjoyment. If he calls her fat, later he'll run a bath for her and light candles. If she screams at him for watching a porn actress, blonde, blue-eyed, she being neither, she'll accept his apology. She knows she's a way station for him between his mother/grandmother and whomever he chooses next. She puts extra time in at the gym and buys a book off Amazon on women learning to love themselves.

My Dream Is Yours

Anna stood on a highway with roaring traffic. She said to the woman, "I can't hear you!" The woman said clearly, "You can still be loved!" Anna woke up.

Now she could go on. Abuse and loss were down the memory hole, dawns and whisperings too in the Oslo cold under a shared vacation blanket like an x-ray protector, refrigerator magnets, Saturday morning squalor, icing on Christmas cookies.

Now she could leave New York. She'd done a good job. She can leave Van Gogh's "Irises," and supervisors, another graduate school degree, men who text but don't talk. Weight Watchers and the cybercaliphate could terrorize her elsewhere.

She would be seventy-five all of a sudden. Her dream this morning also told her there would be another dream some morning that would say to her, "You've had it," and she would wake up that morning, one of the last, and know that she had had it. Clarity.

It probably, the clarity, had to do with the global triumph of capitalism. It was all one *Lebenswelt* now. We were all one person now, in different stages of the story, the same person, some part of whom ruled while another part labored and a third couldn't do either any longer and was sliced off the salami roll and dropped, a disk of facial meat with a horror expression on it, down down down.

At eighteen Anna had had a job at K-Mart and been trained after each purchase to say, "Thank you for shopping K-Mart," and had said with a smile to each customer, "Fuck you for shopping K-Mart," and never once had been listened to, that was her young womanhood. The rest of her life has been detailed. Anna is glad to have the truth in clear dreams. She had gone to so many conferences, sessions, psychologicathons, with so many power point bits of wisdom in the handouts, fit only for the round file. But her dreams were listening to her.

We Have a Pie

Three Thin People

I bump into my friend on the street. We exchange the news of the day, both telling each other everything is going to be all right. The inevitable fat people mill around us. We're supposed to think they're acceptable. That's supposed to accrue to our humanity. But I should mention neither of us has the ability to love, in fact we can't even tolerate others, but on the other hand our needs are unmet too. Various horrifyingly fat people go past, and I am amazed. Many of them are young. It's the first warm day of the year. Every year they only get fatter. I'm supposed to look at this suet parade as if it's normal, as if it's the very best which could be come up with. It isn't, and I'm not so desperately exhausted that I cannot summon up the misanthropy the twenty-first century requires. It was good to see my friend in that we share the love-withholding temperament. We have both been given pleasant speaking voices into the bargain, and it's a pleasure for us to hear them. We could each speak all day about fat, going up and down the streets: "Welcome to the future!", "It's a race to the bottom!", "It's a funhouse after all!" Then we say, again, in conclusion, because we're human too, that everything's going to be all right. We each move on with our day. I don't care where my friend is going. I lie on my bed. The phone rings. Another friend, who gave birth on the West Coast, calls with her baby at her breast saying she's bought *The Art of Loving* for fifty cents at a flea market to see what can be gleaned for her marriage. Then she says the real problem is she's too tired to love. I say to her that if there's a need for Art to get any of us to a better place, she might as well consign the book to the flames. She says her husband says he'd like to stay home and play with the kid all day rather than work, and we agree that seems rather inauthentic of him. She has a pleasant speaking voice too. The baby begins to cry; she has to go. I lie on my back and my stomach feels like it's a nub at the base of my spine, and I reflect that my two friends and I are the only thin people in the world I know. The jury is out on the baby.

*

The Secret of Arson

Her hair was twisted with different pieces running into each other, springy vitality. Her voice was patient and soothing. It was really her style that was delightful, rather than the content, which was her comfort level with murderers. It was a presentation for non-profit caregivers on a questionnaire assessing violence. If people had caused death but were not currently activated to do so, she was comfortable enough with them. She wasn't, she said, as comfortable with arsonists for some reason, but perhaps she needed more training. Her patience was not endless with the ones who wanted tales of a bestiary, lurid questions about the psychiatrically institutionalized, monster lore ~ there would be a sudden hitting of her paper against her leg and a second's pause before the gentle voice would begin again.

Her lower lip was full and smooth. A particular man noticed. Her figure was graceful, and she seemed to be at ease with that. She answered his question about dealing with schizophrenic patients who self-medicate with the most effective substance to quiet auditory hallucinations, heroin, and what happens when these patients with their psychoses now masked by heroin are put in medically managed, not medically monitored, inpatient treatment, since heroin withdrawal is severe but manageable, but the psychosis should make them candidates for monitoring. She smiled and said bad assessment with that happened all the time, and when it did, the patient was transferred to a psych ward for responsible care. Their eyes mirrored each other, and what had been something about tending to damage become sudden love. He knew this was the closest to civilized adulthood to be found in the present time. They could neglect the unanswered question of arson for a time. He saw no ring on her hand. He planned what to say when he went up to her at the end of the presentation. His lower lip seemed to be growing smoother by the second.

Running the Race

There is a van full of lesbians going north to New Hampshire to run a forty-eight mile Ironman race. One of them takes the sports philosophy towards her body, "If it feels bad, tape it." She wonders what will happen to her body when she's fifty, but she propels herself forward, sore bodies are strength.

There is an older woman among them, and she has collapsed on races before; but she is wanted among them, they all want each of them among them, yet some worry she will fold up during her part of the race. Others will not think about it. They are a team.

There is a young lesbian who's new to them ~ she bursts into tears upstate and says she can't, she can't, she's never even kissed a girl. The workhorse of the group knows that they've all been where this young one now is, and anyone who denies it is simply a dirty dog. Her toned muscles spiral as she moves to join the freaked one in a talk, and, starting with the driver who keeps her eyes on the road, none make cheap mention ~ they live their code.

By Newburgh no member of the Bush family has a ball left, except Barbara, and it's too hairy. More than one team member longs for violent revolution to put the quietus on all the oligarchs, D and R. Will a shot never be fired? They themselves can do the firing, or they can continue to run races.

It's about pancakes and oatmeal with butter and all the health bars imaginable. It gets hotter and hotter each year, even in New England. There is a queer therapist among them who longs to start a clinic for her people, but now they are so poor, nothing is left for their mental health, she supposes she has to keep waiting for people to matter again. The roads are potted all the way back to the city.

We Have a Pie

Anxiety Attack

My coworker was sitting at his desk weeping with an anxiety attack. This was the second anxiety attack of his life, and it seemed to have come on more easily this time than the last one of four days ago. Was his brain becoming hard-wired to a new default of puddled mania? He said he had to go home. It was a slow day, and his livelihood was not in danger from it, but of course all our livelihoods are always in danger all the time, which is probably a part, but only a part, of this morning's morning breakdown.

Other times I've heard him singing idly to himself in his cube. If someone can sing idly and harmlessly like a young child and also decompensate in the same workplace weeping in helpless distress, then we're all in danger, or may I be bold enough to aver that I am in danger.

I looked up anxiety attack on the Internet. You take Xanax and concentrate on your breath. After you're stoned on pills and not hyper-ventilating, it's anybody's guess as to the next move. I could list out my coworker's right to have a slowdown meltdown breakdown, but anyone can fill in those blanks under the heading love work body family future past present. If not this year some year some time soon it's time to lose your mother, your job, your teeth, your ass shape, forget your name, remember your past, but I mean really remember it as you see it reflected in the mirror one gritty grinding morning, and then move on to your job where too much is expected and not enough can be delivered, and you weep in front of me.

He says he feels weird. He says he's afraid. If he glanced down a part of a second after a nuclear bomb detonated, he could see his hand turn into mere skeleton. Big picture, we all vaporize together and know that bilked retirement benefits, no offspring, endless lovelessness, slave/robot wage-earning, what have you, are seen to have an end, and within another part of that second my roommate, as micro within macro, learns if he gets his personal immortality with heretofore only anxiety seemingly endless.

*

Damnation

Faust and Gretchen had to take off their clothes in the hell scene. Neither of their pubic regions was entrancing, but out of reflexive emotion to forbidden sights, Alan did forget to notice if either of the two archetypes wore shoes. It was one of those theater pieces where everyone is too funny-looking to make it in the movies and Mephistopheles is gay with a lisp, expected effortlessly to be the Evil One. The actor didn't seem to give a damn about his performance, but then it seemed to Alan he hadn't given a damn about his performance as shaman Harold in *Boys in the Band* a few years ago either. In the hell scene Alan lost track of the devil because other naked people, appearing suddenly, male and female, gyrating, had belted-on artificial penises except for Faust who had had the real, smaller, deal. But losing track didn't matter. In fact, nothing mattered. Lines were rattled out, scenery was bused back and forth, jejune, pomo, and that was okay, because if the scenes had really been played with emotional fullness, the effect would have been unbearable. Souls would have been lost, beauty would have been defiled, death-dealing duels would have been fought, babies drowned, mothers shamed into early graves, gleeful torture, damnation. No one had shone up in a mood to let it bleed. Outside on breaking cable news at the beginning of each hour during the matinee in the tradition of if it bleeds it leads, a truck driver about to be fired from a beer distribution plant went on a workplace shooting rampage killing nine in Hartford, then either shot himself or was shot dead. Over after-theater coffee, Alan praised the matinee to his friend. Not only had the actors busied themselves, but also the audience had dozed in response, slumping trendily in Soho rather than in a commuter train or a 'burb, a bit of money had moved from here to there, the thing had been performed without intermission, and in that aspect resembled life.

*

Hurting

I hurt an immigrant today. He was driving my friend and me in a taxi. We wanted to cross the avenue. My friend got the idea as we neared our destination he wasn't going to cross it. He told him to cross it. The driver said he knew what he was doing. I found myself setting up a cry along with my friend. Even as we crossed the avenue, we continued. I figured out later this was because it was two against one, a safe fight for a bully.

The immigrant said he didn't understand. I said that was because he didn't understand this country, right? He said yes. I said, right, then why are you here, nobody wants you here. He said he was going to cross the avenue, but he didn't understand; he said it brokenly. Later I remembered his tone. It was crushed. I had crushed him. I found I hadn't needed to repeat, as I had thought I would: "Always remember: Nobody wants you here."

In the moment, I had a buzz. My friend and I got out and stood on the corner. The taxi drove off. I smiled and said, 'I have stood up for America.' He went to work, I went to the gym.

Within ten minutes I had gone to my desperately sorry depressed mode. This was because I was unmistakably not perfect on this occasion. I had really hurt someone. But that couldn't be true. I was always the hurt one. This was when I realized I had seen my chance and taken it.

I wondered if I could be honest about this all the way to the end. The end would be when I had served my time.

He would join Al Qaeda because of me. I hoped he would be happy with the decision. I spilled coffee over the rug in the afternoon. God's vengeance. The apartment bell rang. I was expecting no one. He's tracked me down somehow. No, a UPS delivery. My time isn't up yet. I have no idea under what circumstances it can be.

We Have a Pie

Dabbings

It was that extra jolt of liquid nitrogen on February 12 which caused the blister to rise on my left cheek. I became aware when reading that night that the top of the dome was visible to my peripheral vision, a hazy horizon of engorged skin straining against malpractice-worthy water and pus. The doctor had said the spot would darken. She had not said the spot would three-dimensionalize. By the next morning the raised surface had separated out the dark mark I had sought to rid myself of, rendering it into a mottled dusty-looking knob. My face now owned a nipple which my mouth had never sampled elsewhere when newborn. I spoke to my mother, veteran of many nitrogen blasts, later that day, February 13. She said try to keep the blister from breaking. The face would heal quicker. Fifteen minutes later I put in my contact lenses and dabbed gently the excess fluid off my face with Kleenex, and I felt a sudden new runnel of viscous wetness gelatinously oil its way down my left cheek. The blister had burst as easily, obviously, irrevocably as any life dream I'd ever had. What I should have done at that moment was stand on my head so that the pus water could have run its course into my eye. In for the penny, in for the pound. However, I didn't think of it at the time, always just missing greatness of sweep in response to life. Throughout the day I regarded in whatever mirrors I could come to the burst balloon surface forthcoming from my gallant attempt to have a better face. Periodically, more fluid oozed and suppurated. In the plus column, this excrescence represented weight lost, but space does not permit the entertaining of that topic in this essay. At a certain point, the mottled dust skin slipped down a bit, slack on my face, drooped in its waterless slackness, revealing a crescent above of raw blood-red skinless flesh on my face. I anticipated the arrival of Valentine's Day by planning to take a scarlet Sharpie pen and fashion a heart and arrow from my wound to wish everyone my best on the annual love day in our calendar. Thoughts about the final resolution of this situation into a permanent scar seemed premature at this point, as if I would be found guilty of rushing the season.

*

Jiggedy-Jig

There may be a bomb on Third Avenue. 32nd Street east from Lexington was closed off by a cop car. On Lexington I walked down to 31st and on it down to Third. Then Third north to 32nd was taped off. I'm not the type to ask the police questions, but I heard a cop in front of the tape as I crossed Third at 31st say there was "a package on the street." I walked on, staying on 31st, heading even more east, now out of my way. The Chinese restaurant I intended to order from after my twelve-hour workday was sealed off. I walked down 31st to Second, hoping when I got there I'd be able to go up Second to 32nd and get to my apartment on 32nd between Second and Third. People were blobbing along in the street, mildly disoriented at the police presence and the sealed-off blocks, and, I suppose, bomb-anxiety; I barked at some dressed-for-success female who jostled me in passing.

En route in the aftermath of the 100-degree temperatures of the day, I calculated the composition from what I had on hand of a charming summer spread which I might consume pre- and post-bomb. Odd greens, tuna fish, no-pulp orange juice, half a can of Pringles which I had virtuously put in the trash last night after consuming the first half and then neglected to take out and could now with no prying eyes (alone forever!) consume after plucking forth the cardboard tube container of them, to be finished off with withered grapes and Instant Maxwell House; it certainly put a spring of anticipation in my step, coupled with the prospect of consuming same in my top floor un-air-conditioned apartment five days into a July heat wave. By now I'd gotten to Second Avenue and 31st and saw that 32nd was not blocked off ~ I could get home. One of the ghastly stores on Second was open, purveying Diet Coke and M&M's, and I wanted to bring that shop my trade, but quickened my step instead: I was running a race against pig tape. It could go up at any second. The City was alive with bomb possibilities this night, and I might spend my evening at the rim of a sealed-off lockdown sipping Diet Coke and popping candies into my cakehole as if I didn't have a care. And so the war on terror interfered with my giving the cola and candy CEO's their profits this night, and I hoped the loss of my atom of consumer culture might set off the implosion to vanquish the shysty stranglehold on the burned-up planet. What do we have but hope?

I pattered up 32nd now, nearing my home. Incredibly, tape was extended across the street mid-block, but not so far east as to close me off from my stoop. The tape extended across the street, roping off the postal distribution center on the block. Anthrax? I considered what part of the air might be more healthful to draw from. I looked up the street at the more developed end of the block, at the tall blocked-off residential buildings. No one could get into them now for fear of destruction, but many lights in the buildings were on. What about the people already in there? No evacuation of the occupants had been ordered. I supposed I had to count those as among the already lost.

*

Cut You

I heard the police walkie-talkie out in the hall. I looked out my front door peephole and saw five cops standing around with their pads and pens. It takes so long to file a report. My two-year-old played, television on, oblivious. I got to connect the dots. The new girlfriend of the next-door neighbor had stabbed his mother in the hand. Then came the removal of the perp. "You fukka bitch," she shrieked as she was hauled away, yowling to the old woman, who was the only person in the building I liked. I put my child to bed and watched the television. An hour later, the family of the perp showed up in the hall. Revenge. "You pussy, cut you, fuck you, old cunt, you fukka bitch." They milled around, but didn't want to do serious jail time this day. It went on until it stopped. No more blood now. I could have slipped across the hall then with Excedrin for the old lady, or what was left of her, but I stayed where I was. Not that that's safe. People tried to break in last Friday. I discovered it when I came home with Julie from day care. I don't know what stopped them, but they'll be back. I know when I'm on the to-do list. Too bad my husband was a drunk, I'm a single mom, and now I'm fuk'd. Mushrooms are what children are called when caught in the crossfire of drug dealers. Julie wakes up, inevitable potty, back to bed. Windows being not quite yet things only for bullets or burglars to go through, I regard. Moon, Brooklyn, street lamppost, years to come. Julie grows up, gets a boyfriend, he box-cutters me. You fukka bitch. Or I take Julie, we walk out the window together heading for the street lamppost, but only make it as far as the impaling back fence ringing the apartment house. Or I move in with the man I'm dating, knowing I'll never get enough money myself for decent housing, Julie gets her own room, I put up with his presence, before we move, Julie asks, "Does this mean we get a bigger television?"

*

Performance Review

It just hurt so much. I was a half a point away from competence. But my colleague got the point, and she's always late to work and I'm never late. I confronted Poppy ~ I said you can't do this to me. She said I had to try harder. I can't try harder, I always try the hardest I can, I'm not sleeping, I'm trying to learn the computer program, reports are snatched out of my hands. I'm going to ~ I'm going to ~ I can't sleep. I'm going to ~ prove her wrong. I'm going to get that point. It wasn't my fault. I was late to work once, I lied about that, my bus got stuck in traffic. Now I know what to do. I can get up early. I can memorize the policy and procedures manual ~ every day. It's like doing scales on a piano. If I can memorize, I can implement. If I can do the job better, there's nothing she can say to me, try though she might. I'll start with the computer procedures. And I can show her in meetings that I'm getting it and beat my way back to solidify my position. She's not going to get the better of me. I can do this, and it's important that I show her I can. I'm so tired, but I just have to keep going. Drink more coffee, eat less, I do better on an empty stomach. We're all heading for the glue factory, Martha. But I do a good job, and I want a good performance review, that's all I care about now. I want to be seen for who I am and I'm going to be judged fairly. It's up to me to change this situation and have it result in a fair and equitable assessment of my skills. And there's the shame of my supervisees seeing me browbeaten. That's another score to be settled. And over half of them enjoyed the sight. I have to think about what to do about that too. There's a lot to think about, but it begins with understanding that I've been mistreated by this woman, and I'll devote my life to ending that and proving her wrong.

The Voices of the People

Someone had brought a two-year-old to the end of the academic year creative writing program's reading, and that baby had better get used to the piss-and-shit vocabulary of its creative elders, because there it was in all its limp narcissistic inglory. Of course, the obscenity wasn't "over the top," it was the prescribed amount of obscenity, prescribed by writing programs' dream of a common pomo language, "the three-legged dog took a piss by the dumpster on an autumn day as desiccated leaves whisked Zen paths across my windshield" kind of thing. The baby babbled through the poets', fiction writers', and non-fiction writers' quick readings (sets of five writers at a time, 350 words each, mingy treatment for the completion of a two-year program, I think, on a mingy planet, I might add) and though I didn't bother to look at it, you could tell it was a lower-class baby, already beginning to form its words in less than middle-class tone. Well, it didn't just toddle in, it must have been brought; oh, a scholarship student, I thought, gave birth to it just as she started the program, probably helped the financial aid package, but I found myself incurious about this. Still, I confess amusement at noticing fussy audience members abandoning good liberalism at each babble for neurasthenic connoisseur pain, but the baby was the only one producing anything natural in the auditorium ~ writers, I'm looking at you. However, they had dressed for their moment. One wore a funny hat; one wore a funny tie; one wore very high heels and had circle tattoos on her stubbly calves. One was an angry Marxist ~ he said so himself ~ shouldn't he be throwing bombs? One was a former flash dancer (she *said* ~ the one with the calves) ~ shouldn't she be pole dancing? One loveless-looking middle-aged woman wrote about the death of her mother-diva in a car wreck, hoping she had been singing high opera on impact ~ it seemed weird to hope for anything as your mother's life was being snuffed out except speedy release ~ would you hope what she hoped for your mother? Dozens of people, and it was clear that they all wanted to matter with the nugget of their lives. Art, however, is one of the many things which is pitiless. Maybe they mattered in some other way, but this also was something that didn't interest me. On and on, another tie, another cheap brick-red dye job, another bad-boy-via-Darien-Connecticut pose, more and more high heels (chick lit!). A surprise was the ejection of the baby and the lack of protest by whomever was with it. Then there was a short story by someone who assistant-taught at a private school where the tuition was $60,000 for kindergarten. Everyone's ears pricked up at the dialogue to hear how the five-year-olds spoke.

Gogol's Wood

There was a film about Bengalis. The woman was a classical Indian singer who left Calcutta to go to New York and marry a professor. The woman and the man enjoyed marital rights with Indian clothes on, at one point she heaved her arm around him, real passion; they had a son who became Americanized. The son, when eventually it became his time for the beast with two backs, found easy release with blondes, quick slippings. The professor had come to New York because just before a train crash in India, in which he was the only survivor, a fellow passenger had told him he would never regret seeing the world. Actually, if he'd stayed home in the first place, he wouldn't have been on the train to be in a crash; and also in the fullness of time, while on teaching assignment in Ohio, he died in a Cleveland hospital of a heart attack, waiting in line to see a doctor, which also seems a problematic recommendation for globetrotting. Certainly he might have died miserably of medical neglect in India, though you never know, he was privileged. Plus his son lost his soul, becoming a depthless American whose current blonde girlfriend said she 'really really wanted to go to India to help scatter the father's ashes.' Like meets up with like in this world, if it hadn't been one thing, it would have been another, yes, but also there was all that music never made by the mother who instead became a librarian in Nyack. Then the son married a Bengali woman who said she became sexy in Paris and then cheated on him ~ fresh proof of the evil West *à la français*. With the father's death, the mother went back to India, picked up the sitar after a twenty-five-year hiatus, and was off to the races. The creativity of the son was engendered in that he saw the Taj Mahal before college and decided to be an architect in turn to do the same ~ has he seen many Taj Mahals being erected these days, or am I trippin'? In reality, his work was as pitifully pre-fab as was his sexual fate. That was only that segment of the movie, not the ending, I can't remember the ending, but it was probably something affirming. I do remember the father had named his son (I guess the woman didn't get a vote) Gogol because he was reading that author when the train crashed. The movie talked preciously at points about Gogol, which was dull enough. Who reads Gogol? One fact about Gogol not worked into the story was the fact that he was buried alive. They found scratches on the inside of his coffin generations later. It was another part of the world to see.

Son of a Preacher Man

By the time he was thirty-six he was babbling in East Village bars about the importance of Wayne Dyer to bored drunk patrons not even trying to hear him above the din of forty-year-old rock. The seabreeze and Lexapro combo lifted him out of twelve years of music and writings which no one on either Coast had given a damn about. Wayne Dyer was urging him not to look back at the waters the ship has parted in its wake. He pointed out to a man next to him with a Fed Ex package that his old wish for fame was abating, and that now he could relax into the craft, knowing the work itself was so good. Moreover, he didn't need a website, he wasn't a so-called artist who'd formed a band and "here were pictures of my friends." "You're a fuck-up," the man with the Fed Ex package said, "Get another drink." "Yeah, I'm pathetic," he agreed, "I have to let go of my dream." "Don't ever let go of your dream, man," immediately the man said, "Your dreams are your dreams, you can't let the bastards take you down." "But I'm a fuck-up." "That's why you have to think positive. Dreams can come true, and things happen for a reason." He tried to think of the reason for things happening for a second and went to get another seabreeze. Two young ladies were talking at the bar. "The preacher's wife went on trial today," one said to the other. "He called her fat. He pointed the shotgun at her. 'You're too fat to be a preacher's wife,' he said. She had her baby in one hand and still she got the gun from him with the other and blew his head off." "I'll drink to that," her friend said. He listened, fascinated by female lore. "The baby's name is Breanna," he informed the nearer one, "I heard it on the news. The preacher's wife got him in the back, not in the head, by the way." The other immediately said, "Why are you talking to my friend, not me?" "I'm talking to both of you, you're both lovely young ladies." "That's very interesting," the first one said, and they both turned their backs on him. The bartender handed him his seabreeze. He found a stool farther down the bar and opened Wayne Dyer. The preacher's wife was in Tennessee, so it might make a good country-and-western song. There's a murder, so it could be a movie script, with a woman in the lead, so a TV movie, two new genres for him, new beginnings, this is it. He realized as he sat there that his breath was coming faster and faster and faster, as if he were a baby experiencing a fat woman sending a man of God straight to hell.

*

Dance Floor

My friend doesn't want to be the drunk 38-year-old woman boogying by herself on the dance floor. This is slated to happen a few years from now, so she's giving up on California and moving back to Missouri. The men are homegrown there, on the dumb side, she has nothing but the vaguest stereotypes in her mind about them, wants nothing more, thinking somehow people and things are untouched there. But there's "trouble" (drugs) everywhere, friends point out; I'll keep that in mind, she says, dismissing it. She wants to be with her now-Bible-thumper high school friends again, she says she can stop them in their tracks if they broach the subject of Jesus, and then they'll be the same crazy people she went to school with. Though her parents are dead, she wants them there too. She doesn't say it, but I know that it's true. One way I know is her rejection of having a baby herself. "Scunge" is her favorite word for offspring, "I don't want scunge," she says, sometimes she adds, "the little mofo." It's the opposite of her mother's photo on her desk, and yet the same. She thinks if she's a kid long enough, she'll get her mother back. She's gotten wired and tweaked instead. My friend's roommate, a gay cokehead, is a soap stud "about to make it big," he states in a North Pole letter way, but how many of them do? "Mallory, I really love you," he says on the tube, "I want to give you my baby." We guffaw, my friend and I, yet watch it with pangs in our private parts at his worried-puggy forehead. "They don't even bother to memorize this garbage, they hide the scripts out of sight on the set and look down at them when the camera aren't on them," my friend assures me. We have no camera and we have no script, I point out to her. Oh, shit, it's time to par-tay. Later on she slurs something about moving someplace where they have wild horses, wild horses running on the plain, at noon. When they run, they seem so free.

Unemployment

I'm scrubbing my floor so as to be thought inwardly clean. Company coming! The action has whitened my fingernails for now, but we know what will come creeping back under.

The floor is an old one and can't come up truly sparkling. The eyes on their way over to view it will be unsparing. Just how unsparing I am not vouchsafed a foreknowledge of, that would lessen the pain. But pain could wake me up.

I've been sleeping around the clock because in three days I will have no health insurance and I dread having a toothache. There are no signs, I'm just saying. I will have to plead with my dentist to ease my pain, this is what has become of me, and I was born to be a leader.

My neck hurts on the left side from too many hours on the pillow. My weakness oppresses me, but I can't find a next move, yet no primal whispering is telling me this is the end.

I glanced over at my left forearm this afternoon and saw a rivulet of blood coming out of it. I don't remember feeling a bite or wound to cause it. Is my body simply opening up? The running blood was smudged on my arm ~ I've been working the area without noticing it, in front of the television without noticing that either, it's a twofer.

Next, food needs drive me on. Stuff, stuff.

He comes over. May I be excused from stating the purpose

of this rendezvous? Nor can I bring myself to relate all the ins and outs of it, though it only lasted forty-five seconds, with his looking at my efforts, and me, crystallizing his language rather perfectly by saying he is "floored," then leaving. I try to sputter it's just a rundown New York apartment, and I'm just a little down on my luck, but in fact I bypass such grown-up deliberation, and go publicly off my chump, bouncing and jouncing from humiliated child to befuddled no-hoper. Boo to and hoo fro, selah.

It's time to order my unemployment money from Albany. I place the call with my whitened fingertip, and the computer welcomes me. My heart beats pleasurably as sweet money is transfused into me, and my head lolls back as a baby's would who has gotten his fill from some woman the actual mother employed to nurse him with hired milk.

We Have a Pie

*

Audiences

He didn't get into the major leagues, and L.A. neglected his many movie gifts, so, with there being enough money and therefore more chances, he got an M.B.A. and sits in his office making his underlings feel the sting of his discontent. I am one of these.

There's something formless about hating your life and being hounded by someone who hates his, it's a shapeless unspecific scum. No one to root for, as he, also of the company softball team, pathetically, would put it. Of course, with my options, I can always chuck all this and take up asbestos installation.

He wears expensive suits and has a blaring voice that he has a hierarchical right to in these United States. I don't know who he's fucking in the office, but I know that I'm supposed to care. To round out, some role model of his had a stroke and is incapacitated, he makes a point of visiting him and then telling all of us what a great man this was, now in diapers.

Well, he had to do something from his thirties on, he couldn't just die, although I don't know why. Death would have raised him from the ranks of the merely typical.

There was a wonderful bipolar woman in the office, fired by him, of course, but not before her green eyes were pale in fury and she japed at him and cut his funny stories to shreds. She took over meetings. She denied that a great man would want to be seen in diapers. She asked him if that wasn't that true, when he was silent. She laughed at him, not his jokes. He plotted and she didn't care. I loved her so much that I forgave her for not murdering him, for leaving him in a living state, or at any rate a corporate state. She went to Pratt and shows in galleries. I'm not comfortable admitting I'm second-rate, but I'm used to not being comfortable. I think that's my little difference, and I'm an audience of one.

Dancer's Husband

It's the end of the day, I feel like shit. I always feel like shit. My father always felt like it too. That's part of being alive. So don't tell me you feel like shit like it's some sort of event. It isn't, and what do you want me to do about it? I can't listen to it any more. Oh yes you can barely get the words out about how insensitive I am, you're so exhausted, but don't worry darling, you'll manage to get them out somehow. I'll just have to risk your anger by saying all this to you, but what is the risk, you're going to be angry no matter what, you've been angry now for going on two years. And we know why. There is only one solution; I think you know what it is. You asked me to pick up soup? Sorry, I forgot the soup. You wanted me to pick up the dry cleaning? Sorry, no hands free. You object to the cheese in the gourmet store's entree? I took it out, and now you mourn the presence of olive oil on the salad? Olive oil is good for you. Eat the olive oil. It's earthy. You could use a touch of the earthy, of reality. I'm no longer charmed by your dancer's broken-doll body. Give me a chip off the old block. Expand and bloom, go reproduce yourself. Wouldn't you say it's about time we got on with this? What do you think, you're not on life's conveyor belt just like everyone else? You think if there's enough rehearsal room doors between you and the world that time itself won't find a way in? There's a little something under your Danskin I haven't seen in an awfully long time, and it needs to get the action going for the next widget to be thrown onto the conveyor belt. That belt is in an endless motion forward, and at the end, off you roll, down you go, while it moves on under, and upside down, and then up again with a fresh crop from sick and sore women ambivalent about the pitter and patter of little feet-to-be. So get with the program. You're hogging the space. You're trying to run in the wrong direction. You're not going with the flow. I want to look at little cheeks and little eyes and little rolls of fat on little arms. Hey, that's love, lover. You anti-biology people are the living end. Oh, why thank you.

Healthy

Handling (!) one's child's sexuality ~ an improv I don't like to enact. And what about when they start to Do It. Charlene bouncing up and down in the boss's lap for a raise of thirty-five cents an hour. For now, she's only three.

I suppose, as a father, the thing to do is get them out of the house once they've started and only look from a distance from then on. Or until their own sexuality crests and falls. It will. Hang on.

"I have a vagina," she celebrated, crowing, pointing and laughing. "Every part of you is beautiful," I found myself saying warmly, genuinely. Later by myself I thought: "Don't bring down the tone of the planet, Charlene."

Don't tell me this is what she's here for, that this is what all of us are here for. I'm not interested in your insistent peasant slop. She's not sugar and spice, you've beaten that out of me, you can't have more.

She's in love with me. Freud's right. And if she dies, I'll die: my secret. She's replacing her mother. What if the complex comes true?

She gets bored with me. "Don't touch me!" she cries, a propos of nothing, after her baby yoga class. I distance myself. She does her rama dance. I could tell her that to the rest of the world she's only someone else's brat. Now she's rocking herself and purring. This is why they've been squashed, swaddled and penned up throughout time. I move to get her out of my sight.

I give her things in the putrid pinks they want. I send her out to play. She's a good kid. She has her head screwed on straight. Health feels unnatural to me. I don't think I need her to be the way I am.

Part Four: 41 - 50

*

Villain

"Obesity is this culture's concentration camp tattoo," he whispered to me as if I were his little darling, and while he thought I slept, added, "It's the physicalization epitome of a world gone gormless, once barb-wired in place. Oh, those little telltale skin tags formed in the runnels of sweaty fat, each one the flesh peg of a second ~ or was it third? ~ helping. Fat billowings and pillowings are such a self-inflicted campaign of death by excess, are not they, as unsympathetic as the rest of the world now is, unlike the stick-figure *Arbeit Macht Frei*-ers, yes, whom we would have so wished to save, to lead forth from their horror, plying the keys to the gate, playing the violin *à la viennois*. It isn't that way today for what are called people, for what is called you, is it, the Sloth-Macht-Fatsos, the sweet stink broad-across-the-slats-oes. No, you have no honor and you have no identity, you have no work and you have no freedom, where you are trapped is in a food pyramid wherein your vital organs are housed in various cenotaph jars, swelling, swelling, against the crammed-in tops, ceramics cannot hold them any more than clothing, and the pyramid is fat, grand fat, lurid ghastly-gray, leprous, and shimmy-shimmying in a lazy flaccid fashion. Death is the only cure as it was before, but no one is making a count of you unlike them, or if they are, no one beyond the bored recording angel is bothering to read the number, because we all know in the end the number can only be zero, an overstuffed null, a decrepit crippled cipher, you've tried to solve the mystery that way, you've tried a new solution, a new ideology, with a fork, when nothing matters, and for us, the living, as always one thinks there can be no poetry after Auschwitz or after watching people walk on an American beach, but think again."

We Have a Pie

Fur

I put my head in the clothes closet Thursday morning and smelled a stench. That's a dead mouse, I thought, but I didn't have time to dig in the closet and deal. I went to work.

I had off on Friday. I woke and made coffee. I opened the closet door, hoping I had been wrong yesterday. The stench hit me full force. It smelled like a shithouse. Luckily, I had the place to myself, well, to myself and it.

I took out eighty garments on hangers to shed light. I picked up off the closet floor two garbage bags crammed with dishtowels, flannel shirts, flannel sheets, dozens of handkerchiefs, old tee shirts, etc. There it was, lying on its side, its tail like a naked prick, exposed and stinking. The reek struck straight at me, untrammeled by the plastic. I told myself not to retch and retched powerfully. I went for a dustpan and broom.

I'd never been set the task of sweeping a dead mouse into a dustpan before. If I look at it, I'll vomit, I said. I looked at it, had to look at it to position the pan, and dropped the broom, stomping up and down the hall in bare feet, heaving, heaving so loudly I thought neighbors would knock, but none did, they heard all right, but stayed in their apartments tittering. They knew a female Uranian was having a dicey, non-transcendent, moment.

It was rolled into the pan. The pan was tilted down into a bag. A sudden threesome of fat flies flew forth from the clothes closet, active, agile, battened, Eumenides on the wing. The bag was dropped outside the apartment front door on the landing. Forty pounds of clothes now smelling of dead mouse rot was wadded into a nylon bag and left in the hall too for later drop-off. The flies followed the filth. Perhaps things, comparatively, were looking up. I washed my hands compulsively, using a spindle of Irish Spring. Yet I knew, somehow, the worst was yet to come.

I settled onto the couch with the book I had planned to spend my morning off with, Kate Simon's descriptions of Paris, 1966. A book is a journey to a foreign land. Who were all these sleek Lesbians there, with white eyelids and yellow plastic belted raincoats and heels a bit too high for convention, stalking about in *boîtes* or *instituts de beauté*? I've always wanted to be one of them and never could be because I'm the one rolling the dead mouse onto the pan. For instance. I doze off. In my sleep the ghost mouse makes its beeline plunge. I wake up with a ring of mouse fur around my honey pot ~ what's up with that?

*

Swapped Scripts

There was a suddenly apologetic father on the bus quickly making amends to his wife who was holding the baby, something about the baby falling asleep and apologizing for the remark that "If that happened now it would be a waste"; and I couldn't tell if this was one of the new males which magazine articles get written about. I'm always looking for trends, they explain life. He had been smiling at his baby, and whenever a man is intimate, maybe it could mean the universe is righting itself. Yet now in this case it seemed more a slippery slope to unattractive submission.

However, the ten seconds of joy, though admixed with necessary surprise at any position-turn, were deeply appreciated. He had a strong muscular body, in his rising and moving about the bus as the family prepared to go to the park. He resumed smiling at the baby. They got off the bus, and I thought of the other attractive muscular male I had encountered that day, a retired military officer, now a war expert on one of the cable channels.

He was saying to the anchor that pinpoint precision accuracy in missiles would still have to result in civilian death. He had mastered the attitude that he could be strong about this, and he was shaping up the (female) anchor about it as best he could, but with an undertone that the job with her, with any of them, could never really be done. The anchor maintained her persona of asking the questions and appreciating the answers without revealing any of her inner assessing. No new trends, no re-tilting here. Some children had been crushed in a basement of a targeted apartment house in Lebanon, and there was video of their dusty gravitas father with dirty little carried-out carcasses. He wasn't toned.

Maybe if the father of the crushed children were on the bus with them, he would be strapping and hale. Maybe if the submissive father were carrying out his dead family from a precision attack, he would be an emotional giant. It cannot be clear now who are ordinary people and what are extraordinary circumstances. The military expert and the anchor are not people.

*

Parasite

He walked up the block in the West Village where a lonely sixty-eight-year-old gay violinist lived, and imagining his own life there seemed a cut above, or did at least until at the end of the block when he saw a McDonald's. Until then it was a block of thick-painted old townhouse doors, flowering trees in the spring with boughs meeting each other overtop a quiet street with little traffic ~ he looked for an old appendage to a Strad walking a borzoi, the two having been described as similar in appearance to each other, to see if by chance he could know what he was letting himself in for. He hoped the person didn't smell of talcum, it was a smell he particularly disliked. He hoped the person didn't have a penchant for fleshy vegetables ~ avocado, eggplant ~ these made him nauseous. Well, there were so many things. This would not be easy. He couldn't imagine having to eat every day with the person. That had only occurred to him this morning, that it would be every day. It had been a strange weekend of reverie. There would have to be two bedrooms in the apartment. And two bathrooms! Walking down the block, he did not see his new life companion. He stood in front of the building that his friend who knew the sixty-eight-year-old lonely gay fiddler diddler said was the place of residence and was not impressed. There was a doorman, but it looked like a cheaply-made building, the kind of place where you'd always hear the rollicking vulgar ethnic neighbors, but perhaps the upper floors, where he'd been told the apartment was, had large plate windows and terraces, so he tried to picture an acceptable lifestyle overall, some flowers, some dainty titbits to savor on still afternoons ~ his friend, the go-between, had feathered his own nest and knew what a good nest was ~ god knew. And god knew the two of them talked this week about another friend who had e-mailed everyone he knew, saying this was the hardest communication he'd ever sent, but that he was going to have to go back to Indiana ~ some town, any town ~ it was the gay dream gone, that fear-place with variable names of once-childhood-now-oblivion. So: there were downtown restaurants which he saw as he returned to his walk-up with back rent due, in which he tried to imagine *intime* meals taken with the lonely gay violinist on chilly secure nights, meals with the topics of resin and catgut, no doubt, replacing nights in venues where he had always felt so particularly alive up till now. Was he going to be obligated to escort his new old lover to medical appointments a little, so little, later on down the road? Heart, bladder, brain? Something soft and giblet-y? Would he be able to keep the apartment later? Meanwhile, he disliked animals ~ there was not only the borzoi described as devoted, but some kind of cat, reported brindled. There was no easy way now to have what was needed. He accepted having to live with such things now, though he still looked youthful in some lighting ~ practicality had to become his middle name.

Kitty, Kitty

Her hatred of men was not pure, it was admixed with longing. She did not think her large blue eyes, well-toned body, and husky voice were set up as a trap purposely to snap down on male interest, but that was what occurred. She kept herself in a state of pseudo-stupidity about it; it was getting the cat that forced the issue. She stood in the habitat of the ASPCA among ten cats and a volunteer. One cat let out an audible fart before shitting in the cat box. Cat methane stink reached the woman's nose. This cat then wandered out of the box and vomited copiously, voluminously, a large pool flat on the floor that spread out, the woman judged, to twice the cat's occupied floor space. The volunteer said this happened with cats at times. *What times* rose to the woman's lips, but she left it unasked. The cat went back to the box and shat again. It then lay down, not chosen by the woman, and slept while other cats and kittens ringed the pool of vomit and began to eat. The woman looked at one such kitten and said to herself, "Well, it beats a man." She tried, later at home, having adopted it, to cry and protest at the truth of that statement and failed.

She also tried to re-create what she did with men at parties. One time she actually felt the difference between nice men and sex offenders, but the feeling didn't stick. She knew getting a cat was the first toll of the death knell pertaining to everything that mattered. She practiced smiling sad smiles at this while the cat ripped up the furniture. At parties she practiced the same smile while people went about the business of meeting each other.

Melvin's God

"I won't get through those pearly gates if God goes into my bedroom when I'm with a man. I won't make it, I'll go to hell. I've spoken to ministers who don't take it seriously! They say faith and God's grace will be enough."

But he knew what God would see if He went into the bedroom, the ministers didn't know, and he wouldn't paint them a picture. The haunches. The creakings. The night table in fear for its life. God's name taken in vain in joy, in guttural joy. Be not accustomed to the naming of the Holy One.

And God says: What about the smell you generate on your partner's condom or bareback cock more likely, you motherfucker? And don't forget: humiliation is only a cunt's breath away, you're fresh as a daisy right now and feeling so secure, douched from your stench to see Me, but you know and I know it's just a drop of steel-smelly blood away from revulsion in the hair-free Nostrils of the Almighty, and God's reaction by definition cannot be over the top, it *is* the top, it is the top from which you are seen, felt, heard, touched, smelled, and surely shall be judged, damned, afire, yet never completely burnt.

"My friend was my lover. I broke it off for God. I told him it had to be. After he was angry, he understood. We talk once a day."

God smiles and nods: And do you think God has no

memory? Do you think God has ADD? Do you think God has need of Ritalin to help Him focus? He knows about the cum you've had in your mouth, He's added up the grams, and one particle, one scintilla of a drop was too much, add to that one saliva drool column after another in anticipation of man meat, and He is roiled, and, roiled, He raises His bloody delirious Hand to the sky vowing MELVIN (named after the Donald O'Connor/ Debbie Reynolds movie *I Love Melvin*) shall weep, weep for his pleasure ta'en, shall gnash from the same mouth which even once was so a-whoring, MELVIN shall fry on the griddle for lovin' that thing from which men piddle, and MELVIN shall shriek for wished deliverance, vainly voiced centuries in length as simply as an animal's bay, in fact for all time into God's dear Ear during which He mourns but does nothing, having already done all for the sake of this holily justifiably damned lamb, casting MELVIN down utterly unspeakably down into the hopeless endless wide-gated Abyss.

Palatine

I want the crocodiles to fight the pygmy women. I want the doomed children to ride ostriches into gladiators' swords. I want eels fed on live slaves prepared for my after-farce collation. I must be fanned faster and faster. Cannot my torso be hollowed out for a female container to be embedded therein which can accommodate my stallion-husband? Everyone must be drowned in rose petals! Can they not be revived and then smothered again? Send for someone not only to interpret my dreams, but to give me ones which are new. Put the senators' wives in the brothel, and the senators out to stud. Arrange water in a perfect square and assemble all cobwebs. Let me huddle with my morning appetite into a salver of hot peacock brains ~ I feel a chill. My wife shows the first shadow of age come upon her ~ I stomp her pregnant body to death. I fall asleep with boredom at the games, and life hovers with my not being conscious to give thumbs up or down. The swordsmen assume, correctly, I wish all to die, but I crucify them for assessing correctly the mind of a god. Death, death, death. I love Libitina, the goddess of death. I go to her temple. The ghoul-attendants there with make-up of corpse-white wait upon me. We study the death lists of the City together. Too few of them, too few. I want the sweet wine with the posset which makes me sleep the magic sleep and dream the magic dream. I am told by court physicians that if I drink too much, I could dream forever;

and I drink too much, wild at being surrounded by wisdom. I sag, an aureate-dusted sot, on my throne, and see faces who fear and worship and seek, and I disfigure them desultorily until sleep. In my dream I plunge into emerald, cool water, and my shape is marvelous-sinuous, and as I rise, there is just a hint of a poignarded child flying off an ostrich on the horizon. The child is happy to die for to give me a second's diversion. Upon the close stool, I study a man and a woman, whom I have chosen, joined, fused muscularly before me, I like a grave owl ~ this is nature. I let them leave me when fully spent, in peace. The word wiggle-waggles about the court in an instant of my mercy. They celebrate something as meaningless as that, a crafted caesura between slaughters. The inward space within me, miles of margin surrounding my cheated-of womb, is enormous, and I feel cavernous-nervous. I cannot stop laughing.

We Have a Pie

International Relations

It's a big wide wonderful world, so I Googled "Iran Wikipedia" to have a sneak peak at that part of it which must go. Can you name any other city in the country besides Teh[e]ran? I couldn't. I had a quick flick through images of Zoroaster and Rumi as I paged down the article I was too brain-dead to read, and then there were connected links, and one said the President of Iran's blog. My mouth dropped open, and I hit the link quickly before my privilege to visit it was taken by the Department of Homeland Security. There appeared an image of Mahmoud Ahmedinajad holding a pen, thoughtfully composing on a tablet. I still say he looks like the Fonz. He blogged in Farsi, but the word 'English' was there in green, and I clicked on it. In a split second there was a bolded headline with an exclamation point: **Merry Christmas to Everyone!** Dr. Ahmedinajad was sending Christmas greetings to the world, and if he was sending them to everyone, that included me. I was touched as only a once-underappreciated child can be. I love hearty greetings as only a child who was habitually wanly greeted in the shaping years can be. I was prepared to believe his bold wish for my good Christmas as only a child who must idealize someone to make up for early lost illusions can be. Still, I wasn't crushed when a bit later on he remarked that "the Christian message still existed even as promiscuity and perversion flourished," though I got his innuendo. It didn't matter because

I knew I'm a big boy who can stand on his own two feet even if they would be dancing in the air a few inches above the ground in an Iranian open square below my stretched neck. Earlier in the Christmas greeting Mahmoud Ahmedinajad wrote about the babe Jesus held in the hands of Mary, exalted of women. I love the idea that a being can be exalted, but I didn't read all of that, he was prolix. What I most admired was his greetings in this and other blog entries: "Noble Americans!" (I think we're a rather bedraggled bunch.) "Venerable Mother" ~ this was to a lady who wrote that she did not want her son to fight in Iraq ~ wait a minute, was this a put-up job? Had this mother really written? What would she think Mahmoud Ahmedinajad could do about her son? Anyway, he told her the people that sent her son there would answer for it on Judgment Day. On the right-hand column was an area where you could click to send the President of Iran a message. I wrote, "Dear Dr., Thank you for your blog. I like propaganda because I find hope there and only there. I wish we could have met under different circumstances. Do you think everything is going to be all right? I am truly worn out from it. I hear pale brown, the color of withered leaves, is the color of mourning in Iran, do you wear it?" [name]

Eternal Triangle

What did the dog have that I didn't have? And can I handle the answer to that question? I would have sprouted hair up to the edge of my eyeballs too if my father had addressed me as well in that special way. Well, they had a Thang. And the dog's name was Tang. He had a Thang with Tang. I was on the outside looking in; but by the time Tang scampered into my father's heart, I had already internalized, if not consciously recognized, my role as Little-Miss-Alice-Sit-By-the-Fire, born male.

I don't think the dog was manly. He was a dog. But I knew I wasn't manly. I didn't know what I was ~ yet. I knew what my father was, though. He was a mongrel. I guess they had a homosexual dog relationship. My father was the bottom. Tang was a Pekinese, and they tend to be commanding.

I shared Tang's inability to love. What I was denied I could not give. But Tang was not denied love and still could not love. Licks after eating food taken from the hand do not count! So his sin was greater. Also, later, I grew a woman's heart. Even now I can love, though even now have never been loved. As it happens.

Tang gave a damn about certain things, however. You can't take that away from him. His round speaking eyes used to look at me and say: "Stop being what you are. Why are you what you are? If you want love on this earth, you can't be what you are. I can: you can't." I knew what he was saying, and honored it; but pain demanded inability.

Tang and I shared the priority and primacy of food. We each took begging lessons from the other. He whined better than I, but my paws were more limp in an adopted standing posture. My father spooned it into his dish more caringly than into mine. The dog and I both noticed, and noticed each other noticing. There was a dragging metallic caressing sound of serving spoon against dish as Tang's meal was served up, but mine was put forth in short banging reports.

I don't blame my father for his attitude. Tang really was a success as a dog. And in time the very idea of being given a tummy rub filled me with revulsion.

Doctor's Reflections

Not by needles with smack or junk, or by flying saucers of descending fell intent, that's not how to capture a beachhead of haunting import in my world. I haven't been that swathed and coddled, I haven't needed aliens and puncture to punctuate my aloneness. I can look in a mirror at times and dare to see not me but you, suffering humanity, and I think that's a miracle.

I listen to the people who don't care about people. It's such an obvious category, yet it took me hundreds of patients to tumble to it. I only did so when I myself could care about them, which I can when properly connected, like an uninteresting actor risen for a short time to embody significance, being given a good script. I listen to the people who do care about people. Their misery, with relatedness notwithstanding, tempts me to prescribe the big H or alien abduction, but I demur, hoping they'll come up with something themselves.

The essential in my caring about people is to have fingernails not so trimmed that they cannot be dug inconspicuously into the palm of one hand by the other to forestall a yawn by pain as the person you care about talks. Caring cannot co-exist with paring! You cannot expect the person to be fascinating, that's why s/he is a person. I look down at my hands as they appear crossed over each other benignly, the forefinger and thumb of one hand or another pressing crescents of discomfort to the other, and I check to make sure all is covered honor bright.

Hands grasp as well, but I'm free from all that. I listen to the people who want better lives. You're on earth, you do what you can. It's a hand, it's not a shot of junk in the arm. It's a hand, it's not f/x in an invader television show. There should be no commodities, but they pay. There should be no time used up, but I pay.

*

Wynonna

I was having my morning coffee with CNN, and my eye landed on the moving crawl at the bottom of the screen and the word "Wynonna." Now, Wynonna is a woman I think of as always trying to get it together and self-realize. I've seen her on Larry King from year to year. Her silken voice celebrates life in all its evolving wondrousness, yet she has known pain. She is of us who have sought solace in a Twinkie. And found it. Again and again. And paid the endless Shameful Price. Now, this morning, letter by letter, the crawl says Wynonna has filed divorce papers on her husband/former bodyguard who has been charged last week with three counts of aggravated sexual battery against a minor. "Oh, Jesus Christ," I moan. These will be tough ingredients to whip a New Age meringue up out of, and yet what journey-of-the-heart choice will she have? But first, I note, she didn't waste any time getting to the divorce lawyer. I suppose if one simply accepts that all human beings' lives are jokes, it clarifies matters. To put some flesh on that bone, I slap on my usual critique of schools abandoning the Palmer Method and long division drills as leading to the ultimate rot of aggravated child molestation, but I bore myself with this analysis. And yet what journey-of-the-heart choice do I have? Here is one more situation towards which one must be scrupulously polite if one were to meet any of the parties, because it's all so vile. Then again, I have to admit I would be at a loss if

I were in Wynonna's position both as star and woman. As it is, I
fix my intention to look on the internet to research this situation
tonight when I get home from work, and hope I remember, because
I forget as much as possible, but in fact I remember. Cyberspace
reveals. The charge means fondling, not penetration. The man is
being held in Nashville and looks surprisingly old. The minor was
thirteen. The gender isn't given: "Oh, Jesus Christ." It's March
28. On April Fool's Day Wynonna is giving an interview on a
"woman's channel," as I note vaguely from her website's listing of
upcoming appearances. I won't watch. I've done as much with this
as I'm able and set about the task of forgetting. I hope Wynonna
can tune out even more. The minor is on its (I'm left with no
gender) own.

Bipolar Polar

The day after NBC showed the video which the Virginia Tech killer had mailed it, the polar bear cub Knut received a letter at the Berlin Zoo threatening his life, but zoo officials then released a statement saying the cub was "safe and happy." I went to Knut's blog and there were words from Knut in the first person as if the bear had written them telling people not to worry, that he had armed guards to protect him: there was an accompanying photo of Knut and a security guard with a helmet. There was another photo of Knut gumming the top of his keeper's head, furred mouth opened as wide as it could be, eye and ear perfectly round, man smiling below. The only Virginia Tech coverage I heard this day, being on the run, was a journalist asking someone connected with the school whether Cho the murderer had been working out prior to photographing himself with the guns. I visited my brother in his little apartment in Queens. He takes lithium, Neurontin, Wellbutrin, Atavan and Zyprexa. He developed his psychosis thirty years ago. Toodle-oo Juilliard. He has not been activated about the college slaughter. He says after the Amish schoolgirls last fall, the rest is silence. But he's already found out about Knut, as I knew he would. I had thought to bring him some joy when I told him about the existence of Knut two months ago, and he's watched on the blog all of Knut's videos showing him playing. Of course he knows German and reads the blog. He's posted a few comments to Knut, but judiciously. He says to me now, "I hope they don't kill Knut, but they may," with great dignity. Over dinner, he talks about Nietzsche's Last Man again, who, when he sees love, says "uhn," and, when he sees hate, says "uhn." He opens his mouth like Knut with his keeper as he makes the sound, and he knows he does. He plays me a video he's made; it's wiry and spidery as always. He asks me about work-and-love. He tolerates as much of my response as he can. He shows me a YouTube video of a hamster eating a broccoli stalk. We both watch the green astonishingly disappear. It's all eating, it's all eating, he says, and I don't quite think so, but know he must suffer now.

Orderly

I feel the joy of edging paper into neat piles on my desk and of ordering sheets of other paper into task priorities. My hands are moving with authority and precision over the desk against the white paper background of the desk piles. This is my version of going to the ashram. There is nothing on my walls, and my stapler, scissors and tape dispenser are equal distance from each other, fanning out from a semicircle center in a half-sunburst of clerical pride and saucy function. I also enjoy dusted calculator keys and securely capped pens. I need no manuals or procedures of any quality or kind. I know all the policies, and I know what their groupthink rhetoric cannot capture of my employed life. Mine is an el-shaped desk, and when sitting in my desk seat I will sometimes pull out to its full length the top drawer of my desk so that I am enclosed by it, making another side unto me, making a u-shape of holding and protecting by my mother the desk. I spend many hours of most days in this fashion and with thoughts of neatness, precision and intimate metal, and I feel a cubicle bliss in my accomplishment. This is a microcosm of the macrocosm, and from the spheres that I hear are played my life sonata of work and of love. The hanging folders in all my drawers are different colors which make my hands move to the correctly filed genre of work task in a gliding decision of clarity. Tears are distant now, decrepitude has not yet arrived, these are the gray edges from the equal black eternities of non-existence which the white papers, soft-sounding as they are moved on my rectangular salvation, center and mark in the culmination of my space and time happiness, with the folder colors in the side of my mother as splashes of fibrous porous luxury karma, clean, squared, jeweled, set.

A Pink

Sunday afternoon in Central Park and everyone dressed as if they were going to clean the toilet. Well, not quite everyone ~ an old woman and bastard, walking together, he negligible, doddering, shrunken and sunken but with the decency to wear a sports jacket to cover his old hams, and she in a shirt dress figured in small cherries, lemons and cranberries with stems, no, it was not cloth-of-gold, it was not paradisiacal, but it was a dress which fit and her hair was set and she didn't have that look like a madwoman drawing of 150 years ago as so many of her Park sisters did, e.g., the stroke victim in the wheelchair with the gaping open sucker-mouth, a ray of sun piercing and shining up the inner red cavern from which depended a uvula. But even the woman in the dress had a baseball visor clamped around her head at its widest circumference, a sage nod no doubt to skin cancer splitting forth in an ozone-less fireball world. I'd wear a dress too if you could get something like it for $9.99 or less, and the *de facto* sumptuary laws weren't what they are for a girl like I. A cream puff like I. But They won't let me, They hunt me to my death, or is it really that simple? 999 out of 1,000 are too neurotic to follow their dreams and here, for once, I find myself in the majority. Yet have I given in too easily? Couldn't I run a little something up on my Singer for a song and parade it in the Park, cagey enough also to sport a crash helmet to ward off the cosh? I go to the museum; artists know. I admire Rembrandt's Lady with a Pink. She holds that Pink against a dark background, her own body bent and shiny forehead bowing down, her bit of flower in the dun world, and she of course a speck herself. The museum has no postcard of it, I've looked before. It crosses my mind to slash it, but I imagine that occurs to many in this time and place so to do. I reverence it instead. I never mastered oil technique – of course. All the slips and glazes. You know: 999. But I still have eyeballs. I didn't put them out. Seeing is not the beginning of anything.

Cathy's Theme

In the dark in western Connecticut, as we stood outside, we could see the full moon in the clear sky reflected in our fingernails, each fingernail another moon. The air was tinged with the smell of the banked fire from inside. The Big Dipper looked directly above our heads. The woods stretched on, with one flash of a light suddenly seen in the far distance, which my friend's lover said was a comfort. My friend was saying there was only one high school classmate of hers from the little private girl's school who had not survived to attend their recent 50th reunion ~ even when she was in school, she had pulled her hair out, placidly, had a bald spot, was teased. Later, on New York streets, she would beg for a quarter, and my friend said she offered to go with her to the mental health clinic for help, but it was useless. There was no family by that point, no person for her to go to in her state. The other graduates of that class of the school attending the reunion felt the impact of her death, but my friend was simply glad she had not been one who had teased her. Now, tonight, we all three wonder about our separate fates. My friend's lover had tended the fire and said to us now, 'Lead, kindly Light,' and then said she had never read the hymns as poetry and must do that. When none of us spoke, the silence was so total it held us in our contained hush like a space capsule, piloting us straight to the center of the inferred near-square made by the stars of the Big Dipper. Baldspotted Cathy in her plaid skirt and blazer on her way to school from her old parents' apartment, couldn't use New York as a myth of all people together warding off nature, foraging with tautness, spending all that had been made under the heavens, with blotted-out stars above. I go up to my room, they go into theirs. The hush cries out for a human horror to delimit it. I lie on the bed and the moonlight is on the comforter, makes it a dazzling white. I know it's only an effect. I know why it was worshipped.

Solution

My son is dead, and when I tried to sleep, his face and body were there with me and my closed eyes. I have my hands covering my face. I'm glad I'm alone.

What would it be like to have other children, to have to serve as some kind of parent this night? I can be utterly still in my bed, things being what they are. I won't sleep, but I won't thrash.

I know the phone is ringing. Though the ringer is off, it must be. It's her, the divorcée. No, no. My apartment is small and cold. I begin to feel terror the doorbell will ring. Some grand gesture of despair; I begin to separate out a bit of strength to use in case that happens.

This was a day when people treated me for once exactly as I would have wished. Even by tomorrow I would be at risk for the counsel of moving on, I'll stay in here, I won't be seen for hundreds of hours, and no one will be present to be counseling, or awkward, fake-macho, flat-out prying. I stopped at the supermarket on my way home. I have enough food for days.

It was with a spirit of deliberateness that I picked out food on the way home from my son's funeral. I drove fifty miles to a store, a satisfying distance to assure I would not be known. Now in bed with every breath I remembered another food item I'd put in the cart. Several of the items I bought not because I ate the product, but because he did. To leave them there would have seemed like an act of denial. Yet I turned my head away as I went down the aisle containing baby food jars.

I notice my arm now is pointing straight up in the air. My chest is very tight – I think my body is deciding whether to have a heart attack. A fan blows on my face. I hear cars passing on the wet road. I'm keeping my strength for the doorbell ring. I don't know what's next.

I think of Hercule Poirot endings. The child did it; the narrator did it; everybody did it. The solution: you knew it peripherally, but that wasn't good enough, you hadn't gotten yourself to the core of the mystery. Now I have my own case. Nobody did it. It just happened one day. I've solved it myself, with no clues.

The Meaning of Bennett Cerf

The bad news today is mitigated by the presence of Bennett Cerf on the Game Show Network at 4 a.m. starring on the panel of *What's My Line* along with Arlene Francis, Dorothy Kilgallen and a revolving fourth guest, male. The women's gowns, hair and jewels all beyond the beyond of course, yet in proper aesthetics, expressiveness outshines mere beauty, and so it is Cerf's soigné worldliness, his civility and acceptance of the mystery of the line of each guest brought to the 1955 stage which wins the bays, laurel wreath, or other classical foliage which he would assuredly know the lore of and explain in a pellucid manner to others so eager to learn and respectful to him who knew.

The panelists' masks are all on for the interview of the mystery guest, and tonight it's Salvador Dali, whose mustache squiggle shines bright under studio lights with its wax. Are you an artist? Yes. Are you a musician? Yes. Are you an actor? Yes. Emcee John Charles Baker good-naturedly warns the guest not to confuse the panel. Bennett Cerf chuckles and raises his hand at the persiflage, in the grand manner. Wouldn't the panel have known at once it was Dali, no matter what he said, by the sound of his voice? How many Spanish-accented voices were permitted to be heard in 1955?

I could look up the death of Bennett Cerf on the Internet, but I leave the fig leaf on. He died, he was put away some place, the name was slowly, inexorably forgotten. Trotsky would have it that he was well-mannered due to oleaginous abundance from which he lived off the hump of, but I'll not deny myself the pleasure of enjoying Bennett Cerf's behavior and ignoring the roots of it, masked or not, in black and white or not. I had and have the feeling and always will that he would not have despised me for being a dirty rotten cocksucker, and if he had, would have done so in the nicest possible way, his questioning of me on the show done in a safe not personal realm, and the awkward silence at his verdict of my *faiblesse* would last the shortest possible duration, it never even occurring to him to lob nudges or winks to the fourth revolving panel member, male, but letting me relate naturally to Miss Francis and Miss Kilgallen, his remembering Plato, Leonardo, Michelangelo, Shakespeare, the Minoans, the Greeks, the Italians, the Czarists, everyone who was anyone who was dead.

Artists Dying Badly

I called my friend at 10:30 p.m. and then again at 12:10 a.m. Both times I got the answer machine. I was alone in the apartment, and when that happens at night I have to fight the feeling that a murderer has gotten in and is about to appear in the doorway of my bedroom. Tonight I was reading about aging to get ready for a licensing exam, mid-life career change resignation. The lists of deteriorations oppressed me. Nose and ear lobe increased growth late in life.

My friend, years of going through life like a bat-out-of-hell past, had a visiting nurse in his home today to arrange for a hospital bed to be delivered, compression stockings and at-home physical therapy. Pus is coming from his legs. Piss is on the throw rug from dribblings he has made on his way to the toilet with his cane every couple hours. He told me last night he was taking the rug into the shower stall with the cane to be employed as a beater under the hot water, with throwing on of bleach to create an eau de Clorox bouquet for the nurse, but I had gotten the rot stench on my visits. I couldn't take it any more, but we speak every night. We think we're geniuses. Where is he tonight? Maybe he was hospitalized earlier today. The nurse had gotten one look.

I see him wheeled down the hospital corridor. Tears are streaming down his unshaven face. His abstract paintings, collages, and videos are left behind now. The various types who persecute and degrade the sick and powerless encounter him, make him wait, feed him unidentifiable pudding, exclaim to each other about his penis, his pus, his piss. He barks at them, roars at them, but they know he is no more now than a noise and a stink. He tries to will his tears to stop, but tears as much as smirks and cackles are too necessary to a hospitalization not to come true. In his room after a gawking repairman and a thieving nurse depart, he phones me, and I visit him. He tells me he listens intently to the daytime male orderly because he is well-built. I tell him he can recover because he is a law unto himself. He says I can now play lordly parts when I resume acting. He should be a law unto himself. I should be playing lordly parts.

I start at a creak in the apartment. We both live in old apartments. What would my murderer in my doorway look like? I cannot picture him, but I work on myself to imagine him rushing forward to me. All I can see are hands open, all my life they have been searching and now they have found me. My friend and I, when we were younger, made a date in the inevitable and unfelt future to lock wheelchair spokes and die together in a New Jersey nursing home fire; it was a more innocent time, during which we could not know we were to go separately.

Girls About Town

On Gay Pride Day, I went to the revival house and saw *Girls About Town*, 1931, directed by George Cukor, *a homosexual*. It was a film I didn't think I'd ever get to see, but it materialized for one day only, thirty-five years into my waiting for it, even as love ~ you know, someone to love and desire me ~ never had materialized and never would.

You could see Kay Francis's nipples on her pretty breasts in the swim scene with Joel McCrea as clearly as the day eighty years earlier when they had been lit and photographed. McCrea was so charmingly handsome and carefree, probably came from a good family structure and able to live untampered by knowledge of poppers, booty bumps, and the fist. Culture now ill-uses us so. And it shows on all of our uniformly ugly, depraved faces. Moreover, Cukor was very good at creating a suppleness in actors' behavior, so many telling movements and speaking moments, more with the women than the men of course, but I will say Joel McCrea and Eugene Pallette (in a fat simp role) played along too, yet I felt, sitting alone in the second row staring up at them that I made more psychological sense than they all did ~ because if only the script had had one more draft, the movie might have been immortal, and my script is nothing if not burnished to the finest detail and luminous-numinous. Yet if they were lined up here in the second row on a hot summer gay day, the four of them, Kay

Francis, Joel McCrea, Eugene Pallette and Lilyan Tashman, who played the other party girl, heartless ~ I believe she was Lesbian ~ and if they were watching in the audience my life going down up there on the screen ~ I'm sure it's a banal thought, I'm sure that people constantly think of Lilyan Tashman judging them in her brocade with her emerald ring watching a movie of their lives ~ well, I realized I couldn't face it, and I will say for my part I am glad that the forgotten on the screen and the forgotten in the audience were playing the roles they had and not the reverse. I wouldn't do it to them, and I couldn't do it to myself either, I must say, with a shy pride at some scrap of esteem, since a glance from the happy can be death. I see Kay's puzzlement, Joel's shame, Eugene's deep sadness and Lilyan's roll of the eye just as plain ~ I forget how the movie ended, and I don't care on this day how my life will end either. There's probably a book that mentions the former.

*

Adrenaline

My lover died ten minutes ago, and I'm driving him to the hospital. I'm in downtown traffic, and I open the sunroof. He's slumped but not listing to either side. There is no sound like the sound of the last breath, it's the emotional reed of an emptying bellows. He didn't want to die at home and ruin our space for me. He refused to die in the dirty hospital. He worked it out. He knows I trade in the car every year. He collapsed outside the apartment. He collapsed in the lobby. He collapsed before the opened door on his side of the car. But he got himself in. He died by the site of the old Nedick's hot dog stand on 8th Street and 6th Avenue. I recall a bit of string was always retained at the end of a Zum Zum hot dog, like an umbilical cord. I look up at the sky through the sun roof and hope there's some extraterrestrial taking note and going to do something sometime soon for him and me. I park at the hospital and find out, it being the case when you've brought a body, what is to happen next. They won't touch it. "Give me a wheelchair," I say. They issue me a wheelchair, and I count on adrenaline. There's a woman in the parking area making traffic cop arm signals in response to me as I pilot him in the only moving vehicle, which seems heavy-handed on the part of life, but it's like that. I have the adrenaline I need. I wheel him into the emergency room and a man there calls out like a diner order, "D.O.A." I am questioned. The body has to go to Ohio.

The body was Jewish. Now there are more procedures, but the adrenaline is leaving me, and I remember mere shards of hospital surroundings: I saw someone else's stab wound, someone handed me a doughnut, there was sunlight landing in my lover's dead eye. Time passes. I can stay in my home, I do sell the car, I want to practice terrorism on the hospital staff and know I won't but hope someday someone will. I go to a monastery upstate for three weeks, it serves vegetables, and I bring Japanese origami with me. The best part is when I look up at the sky and then strike a match to what I have made.

*

Mitteleuropa

It was my last morning in Hampstead, and I was taking pictures in the sunshine when I discovered the tombstone of Anton Walbrook. *J'adore le passé*, he said at the beginning of *La Ronde*, and I thought of his soft face ~ the grave had "Actor" carved at the top of it so that no mistake could be made, then his actor name, then his original Austrian name, and then it said Our Dear Friend. Appalling to catch sight of a grave with a name you recognize as you go down a hill walking by a churchyard thousands of miles from home ~ *there's* the body! He had been buried right at the edge: was it with an intention that even here an actor should be seen, be put in the front? And I knew that within an hour ~ much less, of course ~ I would forget the feeling, go back to the wonderful little hotel to have my last breakfast because I must be on my way by 11:00, and there was the cultivated Italian woman chatting with me in the breakfast room about to be on her way back to Umbria via Roma and laughing because of the millions who were going to have to be gotten through *en route*, cramming and jamming, she said roguishly, for the first mass to be said by the Hitler Youth Pope. Anton's original Austrian first name had been Adolf. When I got home to New York, a headline said the conservative Pope had had his attitudes hardened by the Sixties. Painful to be bitter after all these years, I think, and if his story is that it was the Sixties, not the Thirties, then he should stick to it, even if folk wisdom has it that as the twig is bent (even unto swastika hacks and swoops), so grows the Baum. I hoped though that Anton Walbrook enjoyed the Sixties, the young sorrow which made his art perhaps could have abated by the end, and abatement for him in a foreign land could have led to final efflorescence. He died in '67. His friends could have worn lamé brocade and love beads to the funeral ceremony, like Judy, kicky in the final years and still moving well on stage. Anton Walbrook could have smiled at it all in the end ~ he had seen and felt sixty years as only someone named Adolf not Hitler could, the real deal.

My Book of History

My Book of History came from the library, written in the Thirties, ancient history for children, and I remember many of its illustrations in washed-out blues and oranges; one was Alaric as a hostage barbarian child raised in Rome among the elite, a sharp-featured bad seed in furs scowling under a Mohawk, tensed between two lolling cascading-flaxen-haired patrician darlings with bee-stung lips and languid arms leaning against a marble balustrade overlooking a view of a perfect garden, columns and temples on the hills, puffy clouds in the for-now-untroubled sky. When I peered out my window, looking up from my book, my view was a clothesline with ragged panties and socks on the horizon. The grass was greener in the part of the lawn where the dog had been tied up for years. And a taste for marble was only to be satisfied by the slab under which you were dead. So mine was a more insidious barbarism just as mine was a more cut-price etiolated decadence. There is a sowing of the wind and a reaping of the whirlwind forthcoming from hemmed-in lives. It's enacted on the grand scale with emp-i-eh and on the local scale with two-cent-a-day book fines. It's enacted on the cosmic scale too, and *My Book of History* had some of that, when the Lord our God says I want cakes baked, firstfruits and six unblemished lambs, and I don't mean five; and what He gets is incense burned to rivals like Baal. There was Baal in the book, some faded-orange idol with a froggy open mouth and legs wide apart, staring out goggle-eyed while wisps of faded-blue incense smoke curlicued up to him, and someone in a linen wrap below was shaking the tambourine. Nobody gets their propers. We've ~ Alaric, Jehovah, me ~ all been let horribly down. Alaric got to devastate Rome, Jehovah got to devastate Israel. I've raised my hand, but no charging armies were signaled nor cataclysmic bolts released, and from this historical fact I conclude that I have a greater ability to tolerate frustration and being passed over than the other two, and feel the appropriate humility that is my harvest, my history.

Part Five: 51 - 60

*

Criminal

The carrots in the Denny's came in a pool of ghee at least an inch deep; and the quarter-ton mother in the booth across the way fattily said to her son, "Eat your vegetables," simultaneous to my looking at my own, so that her ten-year-old Inflate-O-Kid whined, "But I don't *like* veg-et-tab-buls," and then actually howled, mouth open, displaying an embarrassment of inlays. "You little bastard," slur-chimed in the father, seemingly half-stewed, with cocked fist extending beyond porky forearm. "Bastard" ~ so it didn't have its truck with its womb courtesy of you? And what do you mean "little"? What's big to you, nothing short of a Steinway grand? The "You" seemed personalized, but a dog can be called You as well. They had a girl with them who just kept eating.

My friend and I got into the rented car after this quick bite, and distanced ourselves from Flagstaff, or "Flag" as I heard it referred to, Arizona, and worried about America's fate. But it's still here, more or less, and we're still here, more or less. I, for instance, used to hope for world-wide fame, now I've pinned my hopes on continued sanitation. Somehow I feel there's an open drainage ditch in my housing future. I have to do my taxes tomorrow. I didn't know you had to pay taxes on unemployment, but I found out. All must pay. I wonder how much that kid's inlays cost. I wonder how much it cost to make that woman weigh hundreds and hundreds of pounds, what the father's bar bill is, how much iodine is purchased to address skinned knuckles after various assaults on family members. It all adds up, that's why I keep my life simple. Denny, whoever he is, the Mildred Pierce of the new millennium, is the hero of the piece, probably files quarterly, *or not at all*, maybe he's in Dubai, I'm guessing he's not in Flag. My friend's about to get married and leave me flat, her nuptial window of opportunity has begun to inch shut, and she's no fool. I've had generations of these women now, as Clark Gable had generations of actresses to squire, and for the same reason, summer's lease, it's not fair to them, and what is? I've had cases where they left me flat and I hear of them a few years later in King of Prussia, Pennsylvania, or Simi Valley, California, stoned on OxyContin, donned in a nursing bra. "Don't worry, Mother, I'll get by," Veda says to Mom Pierce on her way to life imprisonment, 1945. We need a little more of that right now in this country, as far as I can make out: you do the crime you do the time. Noir takes many forms while you wonder where the magic went.

Beeped

I awake from my midnight nap, Sleeping Beauty at fifty-one with eyelids encrusted from dried dream tears. Someone's scream pierces the night. The world takes no notice. A lonely cornet is not playing in this time in this place in this noir. I scream, therefore I'm awakened.

They gave me the emergency beeper today and the back-up emergency beeper as well ~ staff shortages, staff burnout, staff assholery, I've lost any interest in explanations. I stacked the beepers one on top of the other, also carrying into the consulting room security pass, small clock, pad, pen, glasses the better to gauge your madness, my dear, and clock face turned to me, your madness is on the meter, my dear, and at the correct sweep of the second's hand, your madness in my presence, my dear, must be drawn to its triumphant, or not, close.

At three, I go to look at puppies in the pet shop window ten blocks away. A miniature schnauzer with the head of a frowning Beethoven captures the attention of a toddler outside, who flings himself upon the window. Their eyes meet in a moment of communication, and I hope each of their brains gets a deeper smiley wrinkle from it. I carry the primary beeper with me, not the back-up, although, true, I could have held one in each hand like maracas and samba-ed down the street with a funky beat, a joyous Big Apple Shimmy She Wobbler. I get back. I've been paged on the back-up beeper, not the primary beeper. My own brain jerks a jolt closer to a furious, yet welcomed, aneurysm.

He's in the reception area in a greatcoat worthy of Svengali or one of those characters Johnny Depp artistically assays. He's standing and pulling at hair from his temples with his fists. I smile like he's a present on Christmas morning, and he says he needs OxyContin now, he's been in a car wreck. Well, who doesn't and who hasn't? We don't have it here, I say ~ we've gone to a room now ~ he says I've run out. Where *had* you gotten it, I prompted. I can't go back there, some story. Wellbutrin caused sexual dysfunction, he stopped it. This lunatic has a sexual life, and I don't? Plus horns make him crawl into himself. People at the diner are in league. This little buckaroo needs the hospital admitting room and no denying, a block away from the puppy store by the way, that's the place to get pilled up when life is not an option, and he knows the venue when I suggest it, oh very very well. I join with him in the tedium of having to wander to get one's needs met, and each of us wander on, and the hands on the clock face whirl on, marking our various inevitable appointments, barring sudden beeps.

Coming to Terms

I, a mere woman, look at old wedding photos of my homosexual boy friend, and at least I know I wouldn't have wanted to be that woman on her special day. I'm drawn physically to him, yes, I was from the start, and I give credit to him for telling me about this special side of himself without too much time wasted. Of course with our both being fifty-three, it's all a bit sere at any rate, but my prescription for Xanax is evergreen and continues to make me spaced and dewy in the clinches. Moreover, I'm able to keep my physical attraction to him separate from my new knowledge of his homosexuality, it's like passionately kissing the satin edge of the blanket during my sleep, a visceral dream of love. There's an art to the construction of another, such as his ex-wife did not have the *je ne sais quoi* to achieve. The ex-wife did achieve, however, the leaving of his ten-year-old son for him, us, to raise. He's an unappetizing apple who hasn't fallen far from the tree, given to making provocative Lady Gaga gestures in the bathroom mirror and using up too much money for his private education. I am aware that he can do nothing right in my book, but he'll just have to survive me, as I had to survive mine way back when: that's the great chain of being. Getting back to my homosexual boyfriend, he has a big artless stupid-woman smile ~ I think it got to the wife in the end, and it would have gotten to me too in younger days, but at fifty-three there's less to smile about than ever before, and

I don't see, going forward, that I'll be overly impinged upon. It all sounds pretty grim, but still I notice I'm dressing better. I'm giving it a twist. I have orange and yellow clear beads twined around my wrist for a bracelet, Mardi Gras Me. I know the secret knowledge that he thinks there will be some miracle and his wife will come back, and I know that he would prefer this, but my assessment of the situation is not such that my serenity is disquieted. I don't know what peckers he's sucking on the sly, wearing his AussieBum briefy briefs, codpiece he, codpiece they. Is all this what I want for myself? The down low is a new one on me, but the man not being good enough is the oldest story of them all. Here's something nice ~ this isn't the usual husband or the usual boyfriend ~ so rather than to my woman friends, I can bring the problem to him! The two of us can battle it through, he's not a man, we can make fudge, each knit a stockin', and have a good cry together. Meanwhile, it's passable sex. I deserve a little happiness at this point, and that's just what I'll get, very little.

*

Human Resources

Arthritis in the neck. Armpit waddle flesh packed back behind tank top, beneath necessarily flowing silk overshirt. Gray roots shriek their eighth-inch shine under fluorescents, receding gums increase edge of yellow incisors and canines, welcome to the fifties. And she knows for the future, from her job that she lost doing geriatric social work, that the secret of success in being truly old is to shut the fuck up. You have a chance for serenity. You keep your focus.

She needed to get away from the old people. She interviews for the next calamity. A human resources person has a jar with a stopper on her desk labeled Ashes Of Old Lovers. They talk about the etymology of the verb "to cremate," as well as the drama of speaking the word ~ the human resources person is a failed actress. The interviewee gives a bright empathic nod which hurts her neck. Some time later the form letter of rejection praising her abilities arrives.

She realizes she hunches over, but she doesn't know when that started. Her mother has emphysema and simply won't die. Her father has cared for the woman for ten years and simply will not grow in wisdom therefrom. She, the daughter, tries to eat well. She tries to exercise. She tries to get oxygen to her brain.

Failed marriages, no children, years of therapy, mid-life graduate school, debt, no money, no savings. The landlord raised the rent another few hundred. She's being chewed up alive, and the system's teeth will never fall out.

Young people are a different species now; that implies no envy nor wistfulness. They look like constructions. They have nothing to do with her. They appear not to be sighted when in her presence. She doesn't try to get their attention. She's on a mission. All she has to do now is find a job for a few more years somehow somewhere, and then be silent pre-ashes.

*

Cathleen Calvert

He asked to borrow money from me because he hadn't eaten in two days. I hadn't seen him in months, he'd avoided me. I saw he had lost at least twenty pounds, and having always kept himself trim, hadn't had any to spare. As he was speaking, his front tooth flew out of his head. He picked up the tooth and snapped it back in. He had been halfway through his crown work when he'd lost his job. They terminated him seven months ago with no notice after fifteen years on the last day of the month so that health benefits would finish neatly as well that very day. A friend of his was driving up from Oklahoma, due to arrive with a pick-up truck in the middle of the night tonight. He had to sneak out: the rent. He was a fifty-five-year-old homosexual with no lover and no family. I gave him two hundred dollars, and to keep centered I thought of Cathleen Calvert from *Gone with the Wind*. The Tarleton twins liked to listen to her gabble in 1861, she had cornflower-blue eyes which her bonnet matched, but by 1866 or 7, she was driving a mule cart (I believe), and Scarlett thought while she was looking at her for the last time that soon she'll be dipping snuff, 'If she isn't already, good Lord, what a comedown!' I read the book twenty-five years ago. I still don't know what dipping snuff is. Do you need front teeth to do it? Why do people come down? I left my friend to pack up in the night and sneak out of his house. Cathleen Calvert and Scarlett O'Hara gossip about Rhett

Butler at the Twelve Oaks barbecue. That's her in the movie with Vivien Leigh, the one with the blue bonnet and the sibilant S, mounting the stairs, Clark Gable leering up. The movie doesn't show what happened to Cathleen Calvert. That's why so many people know the scene and almost nobody knows my friend.

*

Hidden Matzo

Were my creaking knees to be called upon to move and get me going to find the hidden matzo during the Seder? The service called for the child or children there to do so ~ hardly a description of me. So I demurred, and the young married couple ~ no kids yet ~ got up and searched. A moment passed. "I'm hearing giggling from the bedroom," I muttered conspiratorially to my fellow diners. "They're in the right room, it's under a pillow on the bed," the hostess said. "If they don't find it, they don't get the prize." "Oh, you didn't say there was a *prize*," someone new to this said. "There's always a prize," she replied. That's not been my overall experience up to now. The young couple came back with a napkin-wrapped matzo. The prize was a small marzipan frog with dot eyes and curl smile symbolizing one of the plagues of Egypt. Many of us during the reading had responded thoughtfully to the reference of the need for forty years in the desert to rid oneself of bondage. For instance, I was fifty-three and had put a gun to my head at thirteen. However, happily, it was a dinner where no one talked about his/her personal Egypt and personal pharaoh. Yet suffering can't be faked and can't be hidden and was drawn on the faces of a quorum of diners.

"That's good marzipan," said the young husband. "I only want a taste and that's enough," said the wife. "I'll twist off the head," he said, adding, "Someone get a camera." "I'll eat the eyes," she said, laughing, and after that said, "Oh, those are good. I guess you can't have marzipan of sore boils." They're working on it. The coconut cake for desert was done with unleavened flour, a complete success. "It's like a cake from Dumas," said a lady whose husband died last year. "Yes! Dumas! How could that have closed!" said the hostess. "It's just what I said to the owner when I went in to buy it! And the owner said 'I trained under Dumas, this is a Dumas-inspired cake, and no one else sees it at all!' We both shed a tear ~ ridiculous." But was it? Because then there was a chorus: "I miss Cushman's!" "I miss Woolworth's fountain!" "I miss Kleine Konditerei!" "I miss the Pick 'n' Pay!" "I miss the G Spot Deli!" "I miss Merit Farms, my God!" "I miss Schrafft's!" "I miss Horn & Hardart!" "I miss Cakemasters!" That was all said within ten seconds. We were missing machines. I gave the hairy eyeball to the young married couple. We'd better get some kids in here. If you're not charged forty years, you have to do something to earn your keep.

*

Why the Paper Towel

He misses his mother. So many different paper products have been pulled out to transfer tears from faces, Dunkin' Donuts dabbers, Subway sandwich serviettes, here a benevolent bit of Bounty. She would want him to be sad sometimes. He said she had been ninety-three, and the subtext was that that was insufficient reason. She had been a good girl.

She died last year. He's moving because she lived across the street, and every time he leaves his house he sees hers. "She latched onto me when my father died," he said at one point, and this sound of grasping to the verb gave a bit of dissonance necessary in a classical passage of grief.

As always there was no one to talk to. What did people do with each other all their lives while they were not amenable to being talked to? Listen: you'll learn something. One got the sense in listening to him that after his grief had lifted, he would not then get back to voting on American Idol, shaking his head at the homeless, or making a dirty joke, but one could be wrong. Some have greatness thrust upon them; and after a time some can slough it off as well.

I sat thinking about his mother. I would never meet her. Their magic with each other was his only. He asked if I had lost my mother. I said she had died two years ago. Hearing yourself use the word "died," one knows why so many don't say it. I didn't say that it was the anniversary of the death tomorrow. There is so much he is not saying about his mother. She becomes a principle of existence thereby, the life-giver extinguished, the source of one's being now past, some flashes of centerless fading radiance.

A Mother's Plight

I knew a woman whose son got gunned down, so she became four hundred pounds. She made a point of saying there were things you didn't recover from. Nevertheless, she was reviled. To her, all the rebukes she received in life from her weight were like catcalls she heard from dimmed figures as she descended a staircase, nearing her close-up. The descent down the staircase however was not a floating one, but a ponderous stertorous one. Her close-up revealed a miserable swollen face, yet one with a little smile cracked on one side. She had shown them.

She saw herself as a monument to a son who went to the ATM at the wrong moment; they saw a woman's grossness. They heard it in her wheeze. They smelled it in her wafting back draft. She had given birth too many years ago to be credited with happy biology, she had outlived motherhood.

It became clear to her that the only way to get people on her side was to go on with the story of her son and to say that it was she who had had to identify the body. This is what she saw. He had been shot seven times. There was a hole above his right ear, on his right hand, four in his back and a graze on his right big toe, looking like something he might have gotten in the bathtub, idling with his toe in the faucet and getting stuck. The morgue, the clammy cold, his sunken face, his shriveled profile, the large drawer pulled out, pushed in. What she hadn't realized was the power of the story is temporary, but morbid obesity reactions are forever.

Then she realized indeed you couldn't recover from some things, but those things were not her beautiful son dead, but her own being, picked off by her visibility to strangers. Her doctors were contemptuous. She was unable to lose her mind and move into fairyland. She was post-close-up, she was back in the crowd and the crowd was hostile. She was too fat to run. She needed a hip replacement. The doctor refused to run the risk. Even the murderer was dead, beaten to death in prison. She was in a quandary. And then what she did was go on a diet and become quite thin. Then people thought she had cancer. Then she got cancer.

*

Woman in Zoo

I passed the children's zoo, walking in the park, and there was a toddler's little exposed bottom in the sunshine. She stood there for all the world to see, nothing ghastly attendant upon the event, clean and adorable, the mother was there, but whatever the story was, I paid attention only to the little soft shapeless fatty heinee. Mine was just like it, writ large, and a half century older, and maybe mine was adorable too. I decided it was.

As I walked, I met people's eyes in the park. I said to myself this was the only hour in the last generation when I was willing to chance love. Someone, if they spoke to me, would be judiciously considered, and, just between me and the park lamppost, I was willing to give all comers every benefit of any doubt.

I decided I wasn't dead yet. I sent out positive vibes. Of course I met no one, but that wasn't the point. I had found my way There.

There ~ life. And I could again. And again and again. And so I prepared to close myself for the day with its waning, like the tulips in the park with their openness, until tomorrow, dawn.

Then I decided, not yet. I walked through midtown. I counted the number of men in business suits. I thought the suits made them look grown up. Most of them were mid-level schmoes, dragging at the end of the day in a collapsed economy in a pillaged country, but if any had said a word to me or crooked a finger, he could have had the whole works, right in the street with all my heart, and a sweet kiss to boot. All mine to give. And I had a lot to give. The sky's the limit, boys, the sky a darkening blue infinity, and a woman bounteous to the world. And I was a toddler too, innocence on two doll feet, wootsie. And I was maternal, to nurture and suckle, by the parking meters, the corporate greenery potted with smears on the side of white pigeon doo, the sidewalk with the gum now black. A woman, you get it? A woman.

I have my moment. Then I'm home, curled on the couch and smiling. I watched my reality shows. Hoarders helped, weight loss melting, treasures found. Them that has gets, the old lady always said, and as always, she was wrong. Everybody has everything. Spread the wealth. Moon. Why don't people know?

*

His Father

I have the choice to be seen as a jackass or an ogre. I choose ogre. I can't go to his fashion show, I can't be looked at as his father. I'm ashamed of him, I wish I could have had one child I wasn't ashamed of. There, I said it.

I hate when Ma says I "ought" to go. I say nothing. The strong silent type. Sighs, a tear.

He won't ask me to go. He didn't ask me to go. I didn't go. Ma and Marie piled into the car. Marie told me he reinvented clothing. I could have asked, "Oh, you put one of his dresses on, and you turn into a human-sized person again, you human Ring Ding?" I didn't. The ogre said zip.

They get in the car to go to New York. I go to the cellar and cast bullets. It's quiet. They won't be back today. I finish casting. I look around. They have no idea what I'll do.

I do what they will never know I do. After that, I have my Swanson's. And what the heck, a box of Cheez-Its.

Neighbors compliment me on him. All the money. But what do I see in their faces? It could make me crazy if I let it. I won't let it. Life is a surprising bastard, no doubt about that, provided the surprise is at your expense.

It snowed this morning. I went out to my mother's grave. The Christmas blanket was still on it. Next to her, my uncle. He was the same as my son. But he had the decency to keep it to himself.

He invented a love story no one believed. Do they die sooner than us, even naturally?

I don't want him dead. I want him different. I'm not going to get that. Ma knows to stop talking about it after talking about it for too long. Well, that's her right. I won't speak here about the others in the town and their attitude. I won't do that because I'm not the jackass, I'm the ogre. When he gets older and I am very old, maybe he'll know how wrong he was. Nope.

Theodore and Tyson

At first, I loved Theodore on *Shear Genius*, the Bravo reality T.V. show about twelve competing (warring!) hair-dressers because of his appearance which I finally realized reminded me of Ryan O'Neal in the first season of *Peyton Place* (I'm old!), honey-blond, pink-cheeked sensitivity, then I Googled Theodore Leaf, although the series did not use last names as if hairdressers have no right to them, but he said his surname once on the show and I found his listing on Myspace and saw his little friends and photos of people who gave him a message, including one from a troll at least 50 (which I am! [at least!! {but not a troll!!!}]), who said, Theodore you rock! and I winced (because I hate it when old people use young language no exclamation point), but searched on and saw a further comment to Theodore which said he looked like Ryan Philippe not O'Neal, which made me feel my age, but then Theodore changed his look for the second episode from honey-blond ringlets to pulled-back greased with oversized cap on his head and skinny arms from a tank-top and he looked ill-used though only twenty-two, so I found myself drawn to Contestant Tyson, thirty-one, who has ash-blond feathery hair and ice-blue eyes and dark scruff and whey face and pale aqua and pale lilac shirts and thick white ties and Sergeant Pepper button jackets (popular in Salt Lake City, where he's from, no doubt!), and Tyson says his mother got him into the business, and I picture my life with him in a way I never really could with Theodore whom I suspect might not be sincere, so I Googled Tyson, not knowing his last name but Salt Lake City Tyson yielded what I needed, has a Myspace posting too, against a stylish Op Art dot background, there was a photo of Tyson relaxing and my life with him continued to develop but I paged down and under married status it said married and he didn't mean a man all his friends' photos were straight men and women if you don't believe me look for yourself I don't need to convince you of anything but in spite of everything I have a question which is that when he won the first short challenge with the mannequin head in episode one and Sally Hershberger the Celebrity Judge who cuts Laura Bush's head for $700 gave him first place why did Tyson say in his voice-over celebratory statement that his mother (!!) would be so proud of him (Theodore when he won the Hair Art Challenge in the same episode said his mother would be over the moon!) but Tyson is a married man if he were married to me you better believe he'd put me first last and always in the dedications I'd insist on it!

A Float

There is a float for the early autumn Polska parade waiting to roll on, but standing still for now, observable. Three young people in two dark suits and a white gown are standing in the front part of it. A sign on the float identifies them as Mr. Polonia, and Miss Polonia. Who is the third person? Which is Mr. Polonia?

Seated on the float extending all the way to the float's back picture are masses of children in masses of costumes, flower head wreathes, red-and-white vests, ribboned skirts, embroidered white shirts, red felt short pants, twisting, laughing, staring, waving, yawning, differentiated eggs. A man there to supervise them wears a white cowboy hat with a red ribbon around the crown fronted with a profiled clawing eagle insignia and the word POLSKA.

The painted-blue back picture of the float has a six- foot drawing of the mater dolorosa with her arms around the World Trade Center, and her halo includes the words in arched gold, "United States of America." A smaller sign next to the Mr. and Miss Polonia sign at the base of the float says that it's sponsored by a funeral home in Metuchen, New Jersey.

Neither Mr. Polonia is self-conscious. A child waving a red and white flag smiles a fresh clean smile. A Mary like this has her roots in Byzantine iconography, and that can't be a bad thing. The man looks sporty and rakish in his cowboy hat. Miss Polonia's long white soft skirt looks like mist in the sun. Not one plastic flower has the same color as another in any little girl's head wreath. The twin towers are not being squeezed so hard as to give them an hourglass effect. The words in the halo *are* barbaric. Some of us will be processed in Metuchen.

Part Six: 61 -- Ta-Ta

Exeunt

When the president of the company announced his departure, the unit leader kept staff in the conference room for a few minutes while the president went off the floor, not to be followed and buttonholed, returning to the seclusion of his huge office. The unit leader could have vamped with palaver a bit to cover up the tactic, but felt disinclined to do so after having discerned during the farewell speech that the president had not remembered his name and did not particularly feel the importance of the lack of remembrance. The unit leader sat at the head of the room next to the now-empty seat, smirking at the human sheep corralled before him, letting the minutes pass before smiling crookedly, rising and saying, "That's all she wrote." Most of the underlings smiled at each other as if they might have known, and might have left the room minutes ago, when such was not the case. The two oldest staff employees, who both reported to the unit leader, had been mentioned by the departing president as "pillars" of the organization, a death knell word if there ever was one, and there certainly was far more than one in the organization, or any organization, for what word in the mouth of an administrator is not a hypotenuse-falling guillotine blade? At any rate, the one old staff employee then characterized to the other, his having gone to seminary school once upon a time, the preacher-like style of the president, that orotund pulverizing stringing together of synonyms and clauses to silence any staffer's inner disagreeing mental chatter; along with the conveyance of complete belief in the unit leader whose name he could not recall, and obviously didn't care that he didn't; it was the same belief which he had placed in his loyal staff which had so sustained him even as he had downsized it again and again all these years ~ faith in, par excellence, the two of us, the pillar twins, pillars lying on their sides, with lichen, he added, pillars from ruins of a now-forgotten time of the company, to be rolled down the hill with a kick, to be rolled down and out for good and all. Yep, the other graybeard said, it's true, killer apes, you got it, how about that. This staffer was a boy of few words and many numbers, counting the hours, days, weeks, months to his retirement pension, which he knew in the event he would somehow be cheated of. And then each in his own way shared to the other the hope for nut cancer to bloom within the ball sack of the departing president, departing or not, and penis cancer for the unit leader, whose name they wished they need not remember, tip to base, death's precious moment whispered to both via cancer of the junk, as if by this they could get back their lives, when such was not the case.

The Gang's All Here

He saw the documentary about Pyongyang and then, near the triplex, watched the downpour through a downtown restaurant's plate glass windows come down and down and down ending the sickening heat wave, but as always with weather now, was it a harbinger of the end of the world? The mass acrobatic pageants in Pyongyang have their display roots in the slaughter of 4,000,000 North Koreans by Americans; footage shown of a military-target-marketplace, a little girl whose clothes had been blown off her screaming and jumping up and down by the balled-up form of her dead mother. The child's genital region wobbled as she jumped and screamed, it was loose on the body in agony: now the taut superbly trained children's bodies move on and on in pageants of garish color, balls are passed expertly from child to child, and all will die to protect the land from American butchery.

He went to another movie in the same triplex after the meal, this time a retro double feature, Cobra Woman and The Gang's All Here. Strange to think these were made at the time of Babi Yar, but there was less communication among the nations then. Of course Sabu's Lana Turner play shorts and Charlotte Greenwood's sky-high leg kicks define entertainment, add to that the cobra samba with Maria Montez gone wild in orgiastic dance, pointing and shooting with her forefinger the next human sacrifices for the fire god. But he didn't think people were being entertained. The audience was subdued, preoccupied perhaps, in a brown study. It seemed everyone had hobbled here on their last legs, the women with osteoporosis shoulders higher than their heads or with hips measuring in at ninety inches, the men with skin as white as Advil tablet bottles and as sealed off from human contact, tamper-proof. To him now it seemed they, we, were all on a double bill too, both looking up at those lacquered performers, laughing tiredly, and also knowing we, we ourselves, were locked in formation to be the new mass human sacrifice demanded, new, huge, at any minute, and which, and this was different from those of the twentieth century, would almost be welcomed.

So Ready

Oh, those last unplanned-for glances of former friends in NYC public spaces. The dancer with dirty streaming hair crossing from Sheridan Square, the artist with his cane exhausted atop a pile of split-up cardboard boxes at twilight on some anniversary of 9/11, the exquisite, once *hors concours*, now in a nylon short-short, legs wide apart on the subway, their faces all either hollowed or gelatinous, wild-eyed or immobile, ravening or remembering.

Then, my turn. My vocabulary is small now. The secrets are mostly known only by you, via my discretion, which I am so glad you allowed me to have. Known but to you. I'm conscious of all this now. I'm not afraid of stillness and thinking, now. It's some kind of peace. If I live, I think there could be more depth. If not, it was an earthen pot only so big, filled only so much, only you know the size. All fullness isn't suffering, this is not suffering.

Do I need to know more? Am I to learn secrets of yours? Is this the time to learn, or later? I know what it is to strain for understanding, and not to get it, and pretend to myself that I have gotten it. I recognize that is not the order of this day. I know I am held. These aren't mysteries, they're gifts given.

I'm the same darling boy I ever was. But now I'm not a boy unknown. I was given that gift. At this moment: no pincers. And if there were, with the ending later of pain, I would return to this, my new baseline. That's true, even with the unshared secrets.

What is the opposite of relics? That's what they are.

I don't think I will ever be discovered as I discovered my former friends, I don't think I will ever be a shocking sight to someone I used to know. Yet all those recognizable decay signs are recognizable because I have lived them too, but not just them. With those, and these thoughts, I could be even more a monster, but I'm not. If they were based on nothing, but they're not. I have a sense of who you are. You know how much truth is in these words.

You don't even need the words that I use, but we are together to me when I put them before you. When they stop, what has made them will not stop. My secrets you cover with a veil. I know what display is and what shame is, but I keep my focus on you, and my coffin is empty. Light has so many meanings, certainly I know I cannot generate it. I have a glimmering. I feel it's enough. I think I'm ready now.

Escape from Angora

Phronsie Pepper sat in a pinafore by a bowl of unpeeled potatoes illustrated with dotted skins as the other little Peppers prepared dinner in a world without brain chips, flashmobs and neutron bombs. The kitchen curtains were fluffy, the tablecloth was checkered, and the family dog sat expectantly, confident in the receipt of her fair share of home-cooked food, rather than being poisoned by the pet food industry due to deregulation for corporate profits. Phronsie, perhaps a shortened version (now that I'm old enough to know) for Sophronia, was my role model at this time of my life because I had gender identity disorder, a/k/a if I were female, I could have done that which would have been expected of me by my father rather than, being male, that which I could not do which he expected, whatever that was, but whatever that was, not doing it cost me my father's love, and I knew it. "Daddy doesn't like me," I said at three-and-a-half, with a child's clarity to my mother, who tried to talk me out of it, tried to rethink and rewrite my narrative to me, but even without my knowing psychosis would have been the result of any yielding, I refused to make revisions ("No, he doesn't like me, all right."), but I could look at Phronsie Pepper and the tied-back curtains and the potatoes in their bowl with a flower pattern and dream. So I dreamed. I had to take my dreams where I could find them, being post-titty. Phronsie had a high top-knot of hair in the line drawing which I used as a piece of what I could find towards the retention of my semi-sanity, and I tried to model my hair after hers, and I realize today, sixty years later, I'm still trying to model it after hers. And I like to think at times I've achieved it. Perhaps as well in some man's eye someday I will have achieved it, and he will say: "Yes. You look like Phronsie Pepper." She was the littlest, perhaps a touch selfish. But I think she had a good heart. All the Peppers did. There wasn't a Judas Iscariot among them. I think the father was dead. (I don't mean to make a connection there.) I asked so little at that time, that when I looked at the drawing of Phronsie, I didn't ask her head to move. If I had, I would have become psychotic and had to go live in Angora, which my mother told me was the name of the state madhouse. Phronsie and I stayed where we were, and where we were, we are.

Phonological

The service sent a female aide when a male was needed in case of an accident. The accident occurred on the apartment house stairway three steps from his door. The spokes on the stairs were farther away from his grasp because of the turn of the stairs, and so he fell forward hitting his knee on the step, his body locked in place with the other leg hanging behind him down the ridges of other steps. The female aide stood silently by. Some other woman who lived above him appeared below him on the steps and said pseudo-expansively "Take your time." It occurred to him to roar that his time was taken and to let his body sink, let it roll.

But then he thought of V.I. Lenin, friend of all peoples. Lenin would have helped him on the step. He would have called him tovaritch. He would have arranged good home care and seen services properly administered. He would have made him an Artist of the People. His eye would have had a merry twinkle at the ceremony, and on his lip would have been a little joke, and his hand would have transmitted human life and hope. During this reverie the old man formed his body properly and righted himself.

He got into his apartment, and the aide mucked in and closed the door. The aide left sometime later, after handing him his 1962 Moscow Tourist Guide put out in English by the Soviets' foreign language publishing house. He turned to "average phonological readings for Moscow": "Spring thaw March 16; The ice breaks on the Moskva River April 12; First thunderstorm May 2; Apple-blossom time May 24; Leaves begin to fall August 26; First night frost September 14; First snow October 28; The Moskva River freezes over November 18; The ground is covered with snow for winter November 23." He had never looked up the word "phonological." It must mean *life*. He knew Lenin must have felt all these events so deeply. He himself had always kept May 24 as his own private, most private, day for his series of images and hopes.

*

Plums

"Yangchow eccentric and master plum painter Jin Nong, 1687-1763," the plaque about someone else said, mentioning Jin Nong in passing, "a contributing influence" to the artist whose work was shown. Seventy-six years with non-shown plum mastery as a result. I would like to see an example. I wrote down his name to search on the Internet. In what way was he an eccentric? Of course, I immediately go to "homosexual," but he could have been as heterosexual as all hell. An understanding woman would have gleaned the similarity of her body's glory to a plum's fold, and loved him for the brushing of it time after time. She would have exulted in each plum painting as an expression of collective womanhood. I don't mean that she reduced herself to a plum, and that happily. But perhaps he found no such woman. When he found no woman, he then became eccentric. All Yangchow set him down as such, except for one person. The empress came to his atelier one afternoon and said, "What is a year's passing? May we not find refuge in wine? Plums lifted from snow. Sudden green moonlight."

Ethereal and carnal -- I refuse to go to the Internet to "search." I remember Lin Yutang wrote that in China once women wore clothes colored plum and men pale yellow-green -- so that plum exterior and interior is a combination of both sexes, solidity, sublimity, and the empress was right. The atelier with purple ink and white silk stood in the snow and in the moon, Jin Nong in pale yellow-green. He looked out at days and nights for over half of the eighteenth century, becoming a master, having his wine, sudden and timeless.

*

The Passion of Phil

Phil's father, on the wrong side of the tracks, used to slam down his gun on the table on Saturday nights and say to the women, "*That's* how I feel about [this issue]!" whatever it was. Phil just drinks. He says he enjoys making scenes, and I certainly hope he does, because he certainly makes enough of them. The neighborhood has a bone to pick when it comes to Phil. When it comes down to it, I have one too. Bone to pick.

I have a cane now, and it's getting harder to defend myself. After my quadruple bypass last year I have to watch my energy level. I don't know what sets him off, but I'm making a study of it. For example, I have a calendar, and every time he drinks, I put a "d" on that day. That's my code, and there's been no sign up to now that he's cracked it.

He's driven all my friends away. I meet other women's sympathetic eyes in the grocery. They think he's my cross to bear. Somehow they'll find the strength to survive pitying my shattered life. Dollars to doughnuts!

I never got used to this arguing. It's not what I knew growing up. I study the faces of my mother and father in old photos. They look as placid as newborns. One cross word and my mother or father would simply get up and leave the house, even in the pouring rain. Then the other would get in the car and go up and down the streets looking.

Of course I have a stronger character than Phil. I threw him out one time and he showed up on the doorstep a week later crying. He'd found some room, but it had no air-conditioning and there was a heat wave. I let him back in.

I don't think he'll kill me. It's more likely he'll pass out and fracture his skull. He lies to his doctor about the drinking. He could never find himself. That was the problem. Maybe he should have used the G.I. Bill. Too late now!

The kids can't stand him. I can see they've spent a lifetime trying to get a footing after he got through with them. They think I'm dumb as a dodo.

But could dodos smile? Maybe I have a bone to pick, and then again maybe I don't. I think I fancy his lined, seamed face. Those old khakis with the oil stains, dirty, saggy. Sneaking into the car for a nip and thinking I don't know. The man who wasn't a man. I smile quite often when I think of Phil and the life we've led. Beast. Secret smile.

Mad Money

Who had stolen the money from the collection plate? How delicious to know, but unresolved suspicion was an exciting runner up. Beth hoped, she said, that the money had been needed for food. This demanded a snort from Paul, who said neither booze nor dope was a known food group. Char got their attention by saying she had not noticed nearly as much hunger among the parishioners as hate. Lucy loudly demanded to know what she meant. Char looked over at her as if to say, "Fig. 1."

Their own private thoughts over their lunch were, of course, more lurid. Beth thought it was one of the paid choristers ~ they had access to the sacristy where the money had been placed, they weren't believers, hired to sing to the old people, they didn't receive communion, failed Broadway singers, helping themselves to wrinkled dollars. Paul thought the priest himself had taken it, he really was a swine vis-à-vis his "little flock," power was his real god, brittle little ruler of his oddball congregation, festering more with each church season, it was a likely enough punishing shenanigan to put them all through. Char had taken the money. Lucy longed for the churches of her childhood, open twenty-four hours a day; you could go in at any time to commune with your God; she was happy she was old; could she just please get out of here, get away from this, get to see her beloved Lord?

Char put on fresh lipstick after finishing her meal. Both

were bought with the stolen money. Her statement had been truly meant, there was hate in the church. Yes, it had been low to shovel the cash in quickly, grabbing it, thrusts into her purse, but emptying her colostomy bag at the end of each day was even lower. Those plates with velvet edges at the bottom and a holy symbol, and with money, were filth blessed, unlike her bag. She felt sick about what she had done, but there was a vitality too. Then again, the lipstick would pass off her mouth and the meal would go into the bag, and there was no Jesus. She closed her eyes for a second; the other three did not notice; she found herself believing that Jesus was looking, then stopping, and she touched the air of His garment, and found lasting peace.

*

By the Banks of the Neva

The aging cranky Russian poetess is visited by friends on her name day, and she snaps out "That isn't a ballerina!,," "That isn't a poet!,," "That isn't a cellist!" Her friends are concerned, shocked, for they enjoyed the dance, the verse, the concerto -- but silently defer to the trembling poetess, rageful in her ruined Petrograd flat two blocks from the Mariinsky. "My God, how we suffered under Stalin," she railed in 1955, "Hitler, Genghis Khan, the tragedy of a People! My knees, my eyes, my hands, my blood -- I will speak, yes, I will speak! Let them come as they have always come, have not I always been ready for them!" The snowflakes out the thick glass windows. The blanket which warmed her still. The definitive bitterness of a genius-woman *in situ*, having no doubt, having no insecurity, *haute* and nothing but *haute*, giving even the Gulag an aristocratic autocratic trill in her brain. Her heavy skirts moved slowly up the apartment house common stairs -- children, cabbages, red star tanks caterpillering on the steps, her silhouette framed in the landing window, she regarding in the white nights departing armies, holy monks stock-still with full-throated chant, the world's oldest promenading professorial couple with their tiny *chien* first clasped to one ancient neck and then clasped to the other for its *élan vital*, sleds of elongated women in chinchilla and emerald peardrops and skin *émaux et camées*, nacreous, czarist, all images adding up and rendering the gray eye surface brighter and deeper and more penetrating with datum after datum after datum. And was once your pale green tulle dress edged with turquoise ribbon in 1913, that magic year? The electric lights burned bright on the white walls by the mirror near which you stood with languorous disdain to shape your look to feline, satin shoes were so narrow then, Pasternak was so tall, you were absurdly devoted to the poetry of Louÿs ~ now Reverdy is tantalizing, there is so much, the picture poem from each window he stood at, the dance and leap there, the verse there, the throaty wooden strain there ~ this is art ~ the fools can't see (and God be praised for making them fools, since I was not made one) ~ but all Russia is art and silence, the industry of the sky, soil vast in versts, waters frozen or flowing, and a hand imprecatory, pleading, allowing, capturing.

*

Applied Eyebrows

When he fell, he crashed against the closet door, which unhinged and fell against the bedroom door, which caved in too. I jumped out of bed. My father, naked, looking up, washed up on driftwood. I know the body, I'm a masseur, but I couldn't get him up, he wasn't working with me. Let me sleep, he tried to command. My mother wandered in, took a look, and walked away to get him a pillow. She does that sometimes when he falls. Other times she tries to get him off the ground and falls on top of him. He lay there with his pudenda unchoreographable, as shameful as the hanging-down genitalia of a pony at a child's circus ride, and you don't want your child to see, and you don't want to see.

His weight was too much for me, and I couldn't find the sudden strength you are given to understand mothers have access to, lifting up cars to free their young. He is not possessed of a child's future. But he certainly has a child's sense of play. He has begun humming "Does Your Chewing Gum Lose Its Flavor on the Bedpost Overnight."

When he finished his song he was ready to roll, and surged up without warning: I got him on the upswing. Then I had an hour off, since an hour later he fell again. This time he's gotten his legs spread open by the corner of his bed against which his genitalia had abraded on his way down and are abrading now as he's trying to be on his way up. Between falls I have told him to put on underwear. He has not heeded. My mother is refereeing the hydraulic lift I attempt to personify to land him on the mattress so that I can go back to my own bad dreams, though I remind myself that no one ever died of lack of sleep, which is a pity.

I get him on the bed and tell him not to move, which makes him move. I have to go to the bathroom, he says. He is deliberately sounding pitiful to make me be bestial. That done, I then tell them ~ because she's still hovering, her little wolverine eyes shining at the scene ~ that I wanted our family to be different from all the others. I didn't want unreasonableness, I didn't want rote uncooperativeness. I begin to laugh because I see what I did want. They just continue to look. I wanted them to go to their graves quietly and obediently, since they were bound to do so ~ and it isn't my idea, I don't want it that way, I'm not getting a bang out of this ~ but I wanted them to go to their snatch of ground modestly, sweetly, eyes rolling heavenwards is optional. I should say keep doing what you're doing. I should say if you want to splat, splat. I do tell my mother, because she shaved her eyebrows when she was seventeen and they never grew back and she has made me say the following quite often, that I will be sure she is buried with applied eyebrows. She wants russet.

*

Kansas City

You can't borrow twenty dollars from someone, it's like talking about illness. I know the Kansas City face, you maintain the image, you smile, you get through the day. I know it and I do it, and it's hard, but it holds up well. It's a good thing to see people smile, particularly when you sense what they'd do if they stopped smiling. So I'll eat the black beans for another day, and the check will come later this week.

In fact, I say nothing about anything at all because the time for speaking is all through. When I had enough loss, I went to a counselor, when I had enough gain I was busy with people, for whatever either was worth. Just as the time for speaking is all through, so is the time for loving, only that's placed further back in time. Now, I have my particular likes. I get a breath of fresh air. I have my coconut pie. The leaf blower works. My face is calm.

Not that I look at it. I don't look at myself any more than I talk. The time for seeing is all through. There are body blows to seeing who I am now. It's not that I consecrate myself to making a great campaign of self-invisibility, but past the bare minimum, I look outward and upward. Earthward, I see there are good regular features on some of the people I see around me, that's not taxing. A neighbor dropped off cookies. It was on a holiday, but I won't identify it, I won't wander in and sit down in the trap of pity. Life isn't tricky in that way for me.

The time for wishing is through too. I suspect the majority of people who have ever lived have died a violent death at the hands of others, even after, as it's written, civilization took hold, five thousand years ago. But that will not be what happens to me. It will be a go-to-bed thing, in the fullness of time. So what I am looks like luck to me. My apologies to Kansas City, but it even looks as if I'll be able to get through to the end without having to have believed in God for one single minute.

Ten Minutes Before the End

I'll be able to go to the doctor. I'll be able to sleep. I'll pay the rent. I'll know a check is coming in. I'll get my health back. Now I have a chance. It's that bottled up strange feeling when good news happens. Good news can happen, I knew the whole world wasn't completely bad, or else we'd all just be clubbing each other. I'm so happy for myself. Which is wonderful, but which is also mature, because I'm old enough to know when something good happens to appreciate it. I'll go to Weight Watchers, I'll see a therapist. I'll start physical therapy. I won't become homeless. I'll pay my back rent, they've been understanding and the retroactive money can go all to them. This is my chance. I handled this all so well. It's good to be smart. They try to trip you up with every application, they're looking for reasons to not give you the money. Oh, I'm so glad, and I feel warm all over. My mother is smiling down from heaven. I won't be poor on this. My rent is cheap enough. I love to cook. Now I can focus and work on my health. The remaining time is precious. I'm at the top of my game, and it's only going to get better. This is just what I needed. Now my life can work. I made my banana walnut muffins and the walnuts on them were like little nut hats. I thought I'd be humiliated at taking the money. I'm not, I'm just so completely happy, and it's a happiness which will grow and grow with every month, knowing I'm taken care of, knowing I can stay in New York, I can shop and cook, I can be in my own apartment, not bound over to a nursing home. There are no bad thoughts today. There is no evil star shining. Now I can breathe. Just to be able to sit still and breathe. Well how about that? Breathe, breathe. I have arrived at my destination for a new beginning. And I'm going to get all I can from it, happy, happy, I simply couldn't be, I'm just so completely

author's photo: Joe Horvat

Robert McVey attended Sarah Lawrence College, Harvard University, and New York University. He is a psychotherapist in private practice in New York. This is his first collection of stories. Visit his website at www.robertmcveytherapy.com